Days of Dust and Heat

During the hot summer of 1888, three men are travelling to Cheyenne aboard a passenger car of the Union Pacific – Luke Tisdale, Marcus Stokesbury and Ezra McPherson. Luke, a medical doctor, seeks to claim the body of his brother, who has been murdered. He also intends to find out who killed him. Marcus, a newspaper reporter from Atlanta, is in pursuit of a story. And the story is Ezra, a man of mystery who once called the West home.

Ezra, haunted by a violent past, becomes caught up in the conflict between cattle barons and the homesteaders who have come to Wyoming in search of the promised land. He faces a choice – either run from the imminent range war or enter the field of battle. He knows that fighting comes with a price, and the price is dust and heat.

I cannot praise a fugitive and cloistered virtue, unexercised and unbreathed, that never sallies out and sees her adversary, but slinks out of the race where that immortal garland is to be run for, not without dust and heat.

John Milton, *Areopagitica*

Days of Dust and Heat

Walton Young

A Black Horse Western

ROBERT HALE

© Walton Young 2017
First published in Great Britain 2017

ISBN 978-0-7198-2493-7

The Crowood Press
The Stable Block
Crowood Lane
Ramsbury
Marlborough
Wiltshire SN8 2HR

www.bhwesterns.com

Robert Hale is an imprint
of The Crowood Press

The right of Walton Young to be identified as
author of this work has been asserted by him
in accordance with the Copyright, Designs and
Patents Act 1988

I dedicate this novel to my wife, Suzanne

Typeset by
Derek Doyle & Associates, Shaw Heath
Printed and bound in Great Britain by
CPI Group (UK) Ltd, Croydon, CR0 4YY

CHAPTER 1

Marcus Stokesbury was on his way to Cheyenne. He never thought this day would come, but there he was, sitting in the passenger car of the Union Pacific, bound ever westward. As far back as he could remember, he had wanted to go West, but it was one of those things he just didn't think would happen.

He also never imagined he would be in the middle of a train robbery.

Years later when he remembered that afternoon in early August of 1888, he knew he should have considered the possibility. After all, he had read about hold-ups in the dime novels. An editor at the *Atlanta Constitution* would sometimes catch him sitting at his desk reading one. He was an old cuss – that was how Marcus always described him. His name was Stanley Wilcox, and he had learned his journalistic skills from none other than Henry Grady. Marcus would never forget him. He was bald with a beard that was as white and thick as a field of cotton after a summer of good rain. He'd look through his spectacles that perched on the end of his long, thin nose at the book Marcus was reading and shake his head.

'Marcus, you're a hopeless dreamer. Just hopeless.'

In those days, as Marcus sometimes thought about it, he was.

For a long time it seemed those dime novels were as close

to the West as he was going to get. But, sure enough, one hot August day there he was, sitting in a crowded passenger car. One of Wilcox's many observations kept running through his mind: 'Sometimes a story will just grab hold. It won't let you go. You never know where it'll take you.'

The story had grabbed hold, and now he travelled with Luke Tisdale, young, red-haired, fresh out of medical school in Boston. Next to Luke sat Ezra McPherson, the story Marcus was chasing. Ezra didn't like newspapermen. He emphasized the point. They asked too many questions, and Ezra didn't like to answer questions. He didn't like to talk much – period – and certainly not about himself. Marcus knew Ezra was not pleased that he was there.

Ezra was one of those men who, once you meet them, you never forget them. It's not that he was an imposing figure – at least, not in physical stature. He wasn't tall by any means. He had something of the look of a farmer. His face wore the lined roughness of the sun. Marcus could envision Ezra in his younger years trudging behind a black mule, a dirt-crusted plough clawing into the hardened earth.

One thing you would probably notice was that Ezra wore his hair longer than most men. When Marcus met him, it was already grey. His moustache was full and more white than grey. If a face can be said to be hard, his was; harder than dried leather. You noticed those things, but those weren't the things you remembered most about him.

His eyes – they were the darkest eyes Marcus had ever seen, almost black. They spoke of mystery. They told you they didn't want you poking around in that mystery. Marcus was not one to mind his own business. He wanted to probe into that mystery. Marcus believed the mystery had something to do with Ezra's past. It clung to him, wouldn't let him go. Later Marcus would discover just what kind of hold the past had on him.

Marcus stared out the window at the biggest expanse of grassland he had ever seen. It seemed to go on forever. But it wasn't as green as he expected. Under the hot August sun, it was parched, almost brown. It stretched to a range of dark mountains far in the distance. The grassland was open. Not a fence in sight, but plenty of cattle, black and oblivious to the train.

'Mister, give me your money.'

Marcus turned from the window and standing in the aisle next to his seat was a blond-haired boy, maybe six or seven. He held his right hand high, his thumb in the hammer position.

'Don't shoot,' Marcus told him.

'Give me your money.'

'Listen, son. I work for a newspaper. That means I don't have any money. You wouldn't shoot someone who doesn't have any money, would you?'

'Bang! Bang! You're dead, Mister!'

'Bobby, leave that gentleman alone.'

A young woman – it was obvious where the boy got his blond hair – a few seats from the front of the car stood and motioned for her desperado son to join her.

'Ma, I'm just playing.'

'You can play up here.'

She waved her hand at him again and he realized she meant business, so he left his life of crime. Her voice sounded weary – and that's how all the passengers felt. Tired and sore and hot.

'It's a good thing I brought my medical bag,' Luke Tisdale said from across the aisle.

Both Luke and Marcus wore suits and ties and derbies. Marcus couldn't help wondering if maybe they should have been wearing something more appropriate for the West. They had Eastern dude written all over them. Cowboys might get it into their heads to have a little fun at their expense. Ezra was

7

not dressed like a cowboy either. He wore a black suit, but no tie. His long hair fell beneath a wide-brimmed hat. Marcus didn't think anyone would bother him. All it took was one look into his eyes, and bothering him would then be the furthest thing from a man's mind.

Marcus pulled a white handkerchief from a coat pocket and wiped the sweat from his forehead. He knew his round face must be red from the heat. Then he turned his attention to the other passengers. Near the front, beyond the young woman and her son, a drummer talked to a family of immigrants. Marcus knew they were immigrants because you couldn't understand a word they said. They had a daughter, perhaps fifteen or so, who spoke a smattering of English. The drummer talked and at the end of each sentence he smiled. She listened and then translated to her parents. On the floor at their feet lay a large catalogue. He pointed at what must have been drawings. Marcus was sure the drummer had come from one of the new department stores in Chicago. He wore a plaid suit. He too looked like a dude. He explained to the daughter that life on the plains now required a washing machine. Not just any washing machine, but the kind his store in Chicago manufactured and sold. It was the latest thing, the best thing. It would take drudgery out of the laundry process.

The girl translated. Her parents listened. They looked away.

Other passengers – the ones Marcus could understand – talked about the homesteads they were about to claim. They talked about the cattle and sheep they would have. Some children asked if they could have a dog, and the parents said yes, of course, they could have a dog – many dogs and cats and cows and horses. They would farm the land they owned. Some produced folded, worn letters written by relatives already living in Wyoming, wrinkled documents of hope they read and reread. They pointed to the letters. It would be good land. The letters said so. The settlers sat on the hard seats and made plans.

'It's the promised land,' one man said.

He was a small man. His head barely rose above the back of the seat. A woman next to him – it must have been his wife – nodded.

'Yes, it's the promised land,' she said.

The conductor, old and bent, who looked as if he hadn't had a good meal in months, walked through the car and announced in a high-pitched voice that Cheyenne was only a couple of hours away. Marcus looked across the aisle. Luke wasn't bound for the promised land. He was on another mission. He was headed for Cheyenne to claim the body of his brother, John.

Ezra appeared to be asleep, but Marcus didn't think so. He was on a mission too – to keep Luke safe, to keep him out of trouble. He had made promises to Luke's father. The old man had lost one son. Ezra told him he'd make sure he didn't lose another. Marcus knew about the promise. He heard it when Ezra made it, and the old man believed it.

Suddenly the brakes squealed and the train wheels ground to an ear-splitting stop. Marcus was thrown against the back of the seat in front of him. Other passengers were tossed against seats and on to the floor. The doors at both ends of the car burst open and two men rushed down the aisle. Red and blue bandanas covered their faces. They waved Colt 1860 pistols.

'Everybody outside! Now!'

Apparently the passengers did not move quickly enough. One of the men fired his pistol, and a bullet ripped a hole in the ceiling.

'Are you people hard of hearing? Outside! Now!'

Some women screamed and a few children cried. Everybody was confused. Everybody, Marcus noticed, except

Ezra. He looked at the men as if they were an inconvenience, something he would have to deal with. As for Luke, there was concern in his eyes – no question about that. He was probably thinking about his brother, probably wondering if any of these men had had something to do with his murder.

Staring down the barrel of a pistol was not something Marcus thought he would ever experience. The pistol was shaking. Marcus considered telling the man that he shouldn't be the one who was nervous, but he decided against it.

'Dude, can't you move any faster? People, listen! We don't have all day! Just do as you're told!'

The passengers all moved as quickly as they could, but it didn't seem fast enough. An elderly man shuffled behind Marcus. He must have been pushing close to a hundred. He kept stepping on Marcus's shoes. A young girl sniffled.

'Everything's going to be all right,' Marcus said.

'No talking! Keep moving!'

The passengers filed out of the car and went down the iron steps and lined up parallel to the train. Down the track the locomotive hissed. A man with a Winchester, his face also covered, sat on a roan. The two men who had burst inside the car now walked along the line and filled what appeared to be dirty flour sacks with money and jewellery.

One of the robbers stopped in front of the young woman whose son, Bobby, had been the first desperado. Out of the corner of his eye Marcus observed the robber. He was covered in dust. You sensed he had been riding hard. Marcus was downwind of him – not where you wanted to be.

'I have little money,' she said.

'You have a little bit of gold on your finger. I'll take that.'

'Please, no, don't take it. It can't be worth much, but it means the world to me.'

'I ain't got time to argue with you.'

He grabbed her left hand.

'No, you don't!' Bobby said.

The boy lunged at the robber and reached for the bandana. The man swung wildly and slapped the boy across the mouth and slung him away from the train. The mother screamed and ran to him.

'You boys give train robbers a bad name.'

Marcus wasn't sure he'd heard what he heard. Ezra's calm, soft-spoken words got everyone's attention. They made Marcus uncomfortable. If a robber decided to shoot and happened to miss – well, he was standing close to Ezra.

'Ezra, what are you doing?' Luke whispered. 'Do you want to get killed?'

The robber who had struck the boy walked up to Ezra.

'Mister, I got to hand it to you. You got more guts than brains. I don't cotton to nobody criticizing my manners. Maybe I need to teach you a lesson of the West.'

The robber raised his pistol, and gunshots sent everyone ducking for cover. Luke and Marcus crawled beneath the passenger car. A man fell from the roof, and dust flew up in their faces. The man's eyes were open, but he wasn't seeing anything.

And then it was over. The guns were silent. The passengers gradually crawled away from the tracks, not quite certain it was safe. Mothers held their children close and tried to shield their eyes from the sight of bodies sprawled on the ground, blood oozing from beneath them and reddening the earth. Ezra loaded his Colt Peacemaker that still smoked. The old conductor, breathless, scampered all the way from the locomotive up to Ezra.

'Mister – you – you shot all of them!'

'No. Not all of them.'

Ezra returned the pistol to its holster beneath his black coat. A rider headed across the grassland toward the mountains. Ezra lifted a Henry rifle that lay beside one of the robbers and raised it toward the man on horseback. He looked down the barrel.

'Ezra,' Luke said.

Ezra hesitated and then lowered the rifle and tossed it to the ground.

'Mister, how did you do it?' the conductor asked. 'I haven't seen anything like that since. . . .'

Ezra looked at him, and the conductor backed away.

Some of the train robbers lay face-down, some face-up. Marcus was stunned. He had never seen men shot dead. He had heard about it. He heard stories about the war. When his brothers came back, they talked a little about the war, but not much.

Ezra fixed Marcus with his black eyes. He didn't say anything. He didn't have to. Those eyes said a lot. They said, 'All right. You wanted to know something about me. Now you do.' Marcus wanted to tell him, 'But I want to know more.'

'All right, folks, back on the train,' the conductor said. 'A couple of you men put these fellows in the baggage car. There's some canvas in there. Lay it down first.'

Luke went to each robber. He checked for any sign of life.

'That's not necessary,' Ezra said.

Luke then checked on the boy, Bobby. With a small embroidered kerchief, the mother dabbed the blood from the corner of his mouth. Ezra and Marcus walked over to them.

'Just keep a little pressure on it,' Luke said to the mother. 'He won't need stitches.'

'I didn't realize we had a doctor on the train,' she said. 'Apparently it's a good idea to have a doctor close at hand out here. Is he your friend?'

'Yes, ma'am. He's my friend.'

Ezra knelt beside the boy. They stared at each other.

'You're a mighty brave young man,' Ezra said. 'You're not

a boy. Only a man would have done what you did.'

The boy pushed his mother's hand away and smiled. And Marcus knew that when Bobby was an old man, he would sit with his grandchildren in front of a fireplace on a cold December evening and tell about the day Ezra McPherson shot the train robbers.

CHAPTER 2

Mitch Harrison sat behind his desk cluttered with wanted posters and scraps of paper. Dying rays of afternoon sun cast shadows of window bars onto the floor. He loosened his tie. He remembered the days when a sheriff wasn't expected to wear suits and ties. He saw no point in it. The mayor, Benjamin Payne, didn't agree. He insisted that Harrison dress the role of a sheriff. Harrison concluded Payne didn't know anything. At least he didn't know anything about what it took to be a sheriff. A suit didn't help him do his job.

Maybe he was just tired of the job. He'd been doing it for years. He was ready for a change. Perhaps he could be an actor. They were doing Shakespeare at the theatre. He could do Shakespeare. He'd never seen a play. But Shakespeare had kings on stage. He'd heard about that. And he looked like a king – the thick white beard, the crooked nose broken in a barroom when he was young and scouting for the army. He had a good voice, deep. It got your attention. Yes, he could do Shakespeare. Maybe he would tell Benjamin Payne what he could do with his sheriff's job.

'This heat is worse than it was last summer,' Harrison said.

His deputy, Zeke Stuart, stood at the window and looked up and down the street. Outside Taylor's General Store the Anderson brothers were loading provisions into the back of their wagon – enough food to last them for a while.

'It seems when we have these hot summers, the winters are brutal,' Stuart said. 'I guess it gives us something to look forward to.'

Talking about the weather seemed the only thing of interest in the Cheyenne City Jail.

Suddenly Harrison felt old. Too old to take up a new line of work like doing Shakespeare. They would laugh at him. An old, worn-out sheriff thinking he could become an actor and do Shakespeare.

'Do you ever think about the way it used to be?' Stuart asked.

'What are you talking about?'

'Well, you know – when range hands and outlaws were riding up and down the street, when the gunslingers were in the saloons.'

Harrison struck a match on the bottom of his boot and lit a cigarette. He leaned back in the swivel chair and rocked and thought. Strange that Stuart should ask. And, then, maybe not so strange. Stuart was young, with blue eyes that shone with enthusiasm. He could imagine Stuart first thing in the morning, pinning the star on his leather vest, buckling the gun belt about his waist. The star, the Colt at his side – made him feel like somebody. He was hardly more than a boy, only three years removed from his family's small ranch in Nebraska. Harrison knew what Stuart thought when he pinned that star on first thing in the morning. He was not just another young man who had gone to town to be somebody. He was a deputy. The young women – Harrison could imagine them – would come out of the general store with their parents, armed with cloth, thread, coffee, and they would see him. Their eyes would meet, and Stuart would tip his hat and they would smile. Harrison could see it. He could see it all because he had lived it – a long time ago. Stuart was important – at least that's how a young man felt when he had a star pinned to his leather vest – yet he wanted more than his badge of respectability. He wanted excitement, the kind he had heard about, the kind Harrison himself had been a part of.

'Sometimes I think about those days,' Harrison said.

'Do you miss them?'

'In a way I do,' Harrison said. 'But there were things I don't miss. Men got killed for the change they carried in their pockets. You always had to watch your back. A man you thought was your friend would turn on you in a heartbeat, especially if you had something he wanted. Those days were rough.'

'You survived.'

'Yeah. I guess I was lucky.'

The jail was quiet. Stuart turned and walked to a chair in front of Harrison's desk. The air was suffocating. The office had two desks, both deeply scarred with black cigarette burns, but Stuart seldom sat behind his. On the back wall a gun case held rifles and shotguns, but they weren't often used. A closed door led to the cells. They were empty.

'That's not what I've heard,' Stuart said. 'I don't think luck played much of a part.'

'Luck always plays a part. Being good with a gun gets you only so far.'

Stuart reached for the corner of the desk and lifted several Wanted posters. He stared at the images of faces that stared back at him – faces of men who had robbed and murdered. He blew off some of the dust.

'I suspect most of those fellows are either in jail somewhere or they're dead,' Harrison said. 'I doubt you'd find any of them in Wyoming. I don't know why I keep the things.'

He knew why. Like the young man who was hardly more than a boy, he too wanted to feel like somebody. He wanted to feel important. And he was becoming an old man, with the dusty trail of hopes and ambitions and dreams that were never realized stretching far behind him.

'They're a mean-looking bunch,' Stuart said. 'I guess you used to have to tangle with men like these.'

'If I had to.'

'Were you ever afraid?'

'Yes, I was afraid. But I tried not to think about it. Fear can paralyze a man.'

'You knew Hickok.'

'I knew him.'

'He was good with a gun.'

'The best I ever saw. But one day in Deadwood his luck ran out. I remember when I heard. I couldn't believe it. Bill Hickok. Dead. It just didn't seem possible.'

Stuart studied a few more posters and then tossed them back onto the desk. He removed the deputy's badge from his brown leather vest, blew on it, and wiped it on his sleeve. Harrison suppressed a smile, but it was hard.

Harrison didn't want to admit it, but he often thought about the days Stuart asked about. Cheyenne was different. It was wild. It was on the road to the Black Hills, on the road to gold. And all sorts of men travelled that road – many up to no good at all. At night men rode up and down the street, firing their Colts and Winchesters into the air. There was music, banjo and piano music, bursting out of the saloons. Most of the saloon girls couldn't sing, but the cowboys weren't interested in singing.

Cheyenne still had its saloons, but they were refined according to the standards of 1888. Harrison found it hard to believe. Hickok had been dead twelve years.

A sudden, loud blast from a locomotive jolted Harrison from his memories. He checked his pocket watch. The 3:20 was late, over an hour late. Not really that unusual. He finished his cigarette and started to think about supper.

The door flew open and Curtis, a telegraph operator, rushed in. He was only a few years older than Stuart and, like the deputy, he had escaped the farm. He had found the excitement of faraway voices singing on a wire. His face was red and he struggled for his breath.

'Sheriff, there's been trouble,' Curtis said.

'What kind of trouble?' Harrison asked. 'Did somebody spit on the sidewalk?'

'Train robbery. About two hours from here.'

Harrison stood. He couldn't say for sure when there had last been a train robbery, but he knew it was long ago.

'Anybody killed?'

'Four.'

'Passengers or crew?'

'Neither.'

'Neither? I thought you said four were killed.'

'I did, Sheriff. But they weren't passengers or crew. They were robbers. One of the passengers shot them. The conductor told me he hadn't seen anything like it in his life. This fellow shot four robbers. One got away.'

'One man shot four train robbers?' Stuart asked.

'That's what the conductor said.'

'Who's the conductor?' Harrison asked.

'Old man Newcomb.'

'I'm not sure I'd believe a whole lot of what that old geezer has to say. I'm surprised he's still making the run out here.'

'I wonder who that passenger is,' Stuart said. 'He's gotta be a gunman. What do you think, Sheriff?'

'What do I think? I think I want to meet him. Zeke, walk over to the depot and introduce yourself – politely, you hear me? – and ask this gentleman to step across the street. Tell him the sheriff wants to ask him a few questions. Tell him it's just procedure. Don't act threatening. You got it?'

'Yes, sir. Come on, Curtis.'

Stuart stopped at the door and looked back at Harrison.

'Maybe the old days are back,' Stuart said.

Harrison breathed deeply and said nothing.

CHAPTER 3

Ezra, Luke and Marcus stood on the wooden platform in front of the large pale brown stone railroad cathedral. They had not expected a depot with dormers and a tall clock tower that reached toward the endless Wyoming sky. In front of the platform, wagons and buggies crowded into the shadows of a barren yard. Farmers and ranchers – at least Marcus figured that's who they were – waited for passengers, for relatives who sought a new life. Beyond the yard ran the main street. Marcus looked at the two- and three-storey brick buildings, some with fabric overhangs.

'Stokesbury, what do you think?' Ezra asked.

'It's not what I envisioned. I feel like I'm in Atlanta.'

'The West apparently isn't what it used to be. It's grown up. At least that's the way it appears.'

'You don't sound pleased.'

'Things aren't going to stay the same, Stokesbury. You know that. And I suppose that's how it should be.'

Passengers found their friends and families in the yard. There were shouts, laughter, embraces and tears. And then, it seemed, everyone looked at Ezra on the platform. Marcus knew the passengers would recount the story of the robbery, probably with one or two embellishments. They would eat their first Wyoming supper. They would put their children to bed for their first Wyoming sleep. And then they would sit and stand in the kitchen and talk about the robbery.

At the edge of the platform the boy, Bobby, stood with his mother. Luke walked toward them.

'Son, how's your lip?'

'It don't hurt.'

'Let me see.'

Luke bent down and studied the purplish bruise.

'When you get where you're going, put a cold compress on it. That should help the swelling go down.'

'Are you here in Cheyenne to practise?' the woman asked.

Luke stood and studied her. She wore a plain white cotton dress with lace about her throat. Blonde hair swept into a ball on the back of her head. Her green eyes were small, uncertain. Like the other passengers, she had not expected to be in the middle of a robbery. She had not expected to hear gunshots and to see men lying dead in the dust.

'No, I'm not here to practise,' Luke said. 'My practice is in Boston, but I have business here. My name is Luke Tisdale.'

'Jennifer Beauchamp. This is Bobby.'

'I'm the man of the house,' the boy said.

'His father is. . . .'

'My dad told me I was going to be the man of the house,' Bobby said.

'And I bet you are,' Luke said.

'Mom's a school teacher. We're from Charleston.'

'Is that so? Why, we were practically neighbours. My father has a place on Jekyll Island. Do you know where that is?'

'No,' Bobby said.

'It's off the coast of Georgia.'

'I've heard of Jekyll,' the woman said.

'Mister, are you going to come see us?' Bobby asked.

'Bobby, you shouldn't ask such a question,' she said.

'Well, Bobby, we'll have to see.'

'When you come, bring the man who killed the train robbers. I want him to teach me how to shoot.'

A woman in a loose-fitting calico dress and a faded blue bonnet climbed the steps and spread her arms wide. Jennifer ran into them, but Bobby hesitated.

'Welcome to Cheyenne, honey. Silas has the buckboard.'

'Charlotte, this is Bobby. Bobby, this is your Aunt Charlotte.'

'Hello, Bobby. Where on earth did you get that bruise? Have you been in a fight?'

'Yes, ma'am.'

'Charlotte, I want you to meet Dr Tisdale. Dr Tisdale, this is my sister, Charlotte Taylor.'

'Pleased to meet you, ma'am,' he said and he removed his hat.

'We could use another doctor in this town,' the sister said. 'Jennifer, we need to go. Silas hasn't changed. He still gets impatient. Good to meet you, Dr Tisdale. Come on, Bobby. Help your mother with the luggage. Now you mustn't be fighting. We try not to do that sort of thing out here.'

'May I help with the bags?' Luke asked.

'No, we'll manage,' Jennifer said. 'You're kind to ask. Stay away from train robbers, Dr Tisdale.'

'I'll see what I can do.'

They disappeared among the throng of people.

'We'd best be going too,' Ezra said. 'Unless of course there are some other ladies you want to speak to.'

With their grips in hand, they descended the steps of the platform and crossed the yard. They entered Main Street, and Ezra saw the young man. Across the street, on the sidewalk, he talked to the train conductor. The old man looked, saw Ezra, and pointed. The young man waited for a wagon to move out of the way and he crossed the street and headed directly toward Ezra, Luke, and Marcus. Despite the late afternoon shadows, Ezra saw the star on the vest.

'Gentlemen, welcome to Cheyenne. I'm Deputy Sheriff Stuart. Would you mind coming with me?'

'Where?' Luke asked.

'Just down the street. Sheriff Harrison would like to talk to you. Nothing to worry about.'

They followed the deputy. Women in silk dresses walked along the sidewalks. They stopped and stared, mostly at Ezra. It seemed word travelled quickly.

'There's money in this town,' Marcus said.

'How do you figure that?' Ezra asked.

'I can tell just by the way people dress. Those women we just passed – they'd be right at home in Savannah or Charleston or New York, for that matter.'

'Stokesbury, I didn't know you were such an expert on fashion.'

They came to the two-storey red brick jail. It sat apart from the other buildings. Stuart opened the door.

'Gentlemen, come in,' Harrison said. 'Pull up a chair. Let's have a talk.'

Three chairs sat in front of the desk. Ezra, Luke and Marcus hesitated. Stuart stood behind them.

'I just want to ask you a few questions,' Harrison said. 'Please – have a seat.'

They sat, but Stuart remained standing at the door. The office was hot, and Marcus removed his hat.

'Cheyenne – indeed, all of Wyoming – owes you boys a debt of gratitude,' Harrison said. 'Would you like a cigar? They ain't anything special, but they are cigars.'

He pushed a box to the edge of the desk, but the three shook their heads.

'We don't have train robberies too much any more,' Harrison said. 'When I heard that the train you were on was held up, I was surprised. And when I heard one of you killed most of the robbers, I was – well, I was more than astounded. Let me guess which one of you sent those robbers to their just reward.'

Harrison looked directly at Ezra.

'I'm meaner than I look,' Marcus said.

Harrison leaned forward in his chair.

'What's your name?'

'McPherson. Ezra McPherson.'

'I've never heard of you.'

'Should you have heard of me?'

'When a man shoots the way you apparently do, then I should hear of him. Where are you from?'

'We're from Jekyll Island,' Luke said. 'At least, Ezra and I are. This other gentleman, Marcus Stokesbury, is from Atlanta.'

'I've heard of Atlanta. I had some good friends who visited Atlanta in 1864. I haven't heard of the other place.'

'It's off the coast of Georgia,' Luke said.

'Off the coast of Georgia. You don't say. Mr McPherson, do you get a lot of practice shooting off the coast of Georgia?'

'My father has a hunting preserve on Jekyll,' Luke said. 'Ezra runs it.'

'You stop many train robberies on Jekyll?'

'We've never had a train robbery on Jekyll,' Ezra said.

'No, I don't suppose you have. Mr McPherson, as you can see, I'm not a young man. And as I can see, neither are you. I should have heard of you.'

'I should have heard of you, but I haven't.'

'Well, I guess we're both disappointed, but life's full of disappointments. I've learned to deal with them. Young man, what's your name?'

'Luke Tisdale.'

The sheriff's bushy white eyebrows crawled close together. 'Tisdale?'

'Yes, sir. My father owns the Tisdale Steel Works in Pittsburgh.'

'You've got what appears to be a medical bag.'

'I'm a doctor.'

'You planning to open shop here? We already have a doctor.'

'No, I'm not.'

Harrison sat back in the swivel chair and drew in a deep breath and exhaled slowly.

'Well, son, do you mind telling me why you're here in Cheyenne?'

'My brother, John, was killed here in Cheyenne. We're going to take his body back East.'

'So you're John Tisdale's brother,' Harrison said. 'Slade has his body. He told me somebody was coming for it. The mortuary is at the end of the street. I suspect he's busy taking care of those train robbers right about now. I recommend you see him first thing in the morning.'

'Can you tell me what happened?'

Harrison shifted position in the chair. The three men sitting in front of the desk stared at him, and he didn't like it.

'Your brother was shot and killed. He had been playing poker. . . .'

'John didn't gamble.'

'I've been told he did. I've been told he had been drinking and lost quite a bit of money. Words were spoken, words best left unsaid. His body was found in the alley next to the saloon, O'Faolin's.'

'Who shot him?'

'There were no witnesses. I've looked into it. Without witnesses, it's hard. . . .'

'So you've given up.'

'Look here, son.'

'Luke, I think we'd best be on our way,' Ezra said.

The three men stood and turned and started toward the door.

'I want you to listen and to listen good,' Harrison said. 'I won't stand for any vengeance-is-mine type of thing. You hear me? This town isn't what you may think the West is. The days of gunfights in the street are over. Just ride around town. Look at the mansions that have been built. Good families live there. Look at the gentlemen's club. The best ranchers in the county go there to smoke their cigars – and they're a heap better than mine – and discuss politics. Look at the theatre. They're going to do *Hamlet* next week. I don't know much about Shakespeare, but it shows how far this town has come. Mr McPherson, I don't know who you are. Maybe you're this young man's hired gun. But I'm warning you. This town is peaceful, and it's going to stay that way. I don't want any trouble out of you.'

Luke bit his lower lip. He wanted to grab the sheriff out of his chair and shake him until the truth spilled out. Ezra fixed his eyes on Harrison, and the sheriff felt fear, the kind he hadn't felt in a long time. For what seemed like an hour, nobody spoke, and then Ezra opened the door, and he and Luke and Marcus walked out.

'Sheriff, do you want me to keep an eye on that fellow?' Stuart asked.

Harrison shook his head.

'He's a professional. He might not take kindly to being watched. I don't want you to get killed.'

'I can take care of myself,' Stuart said.

'Zeke, you wondered what the old days were like. Well, the old days just walked out of here. That's the kind of man you don't mess with unless he breaks the law. Were there a bunch of settlers on that train?'

'Yes, sir, quite a few.'

'That's what I was afraid of. Swearingen ain't going to like that. I want you to go down to Slade's and try to find out who those train robbers were.'

'Sure,' Stuart said.

The deputy left and the jail was quiet. Stuart had a lot of confidence. It came with being young. Harrison was once the same way – a long time ago.

Suddenly he missed Penelope. Suddenly he wanted to go to his small house on the outskirts of town and find her waiting for him. He remembered hearing the word he never wanted to hear. Typhoid. When Doc Grierson said the word, Harrison knew she was going to leave him. And, now, in the late hot afternoon of August he missed her. He wanted her. Evening shadows covered Cheyenne, and he felt alone.

CHAPTER 4

Richard Swearingen stood at the window behind his desk and stared into the darkness. The corral and the barn were hardly visible. Ranch hands, tired, dusty, and hungry, rounded the corner of the house. Their voices were voices of the land – despite their weariness, despite the heat, they talked and joked and laughed – and it was good to hear them. They were voices he never heard in New York. He would have to return soon. He knew it, but the thought unsettled him. There was too much to do at the ranch. It needed him. And what needed to be done could not be trusted to anyone else.

'I'm talking to you, Richard. I wish you'd listen.'

He had not listened. He liked to be alone in his study. More than once he had made his preference known to Ginevra, yet there she was. She hovered just inside the door. Then she came closer. The silk of her dress rustled. Her footfall was light, light as a mouse, yet he heard.

'I'm listening.'

'Then turn around.'

'All right. Are you happy? I've turned. You have my full attention. What is it you want me to do?'

'I want you to speak to Andrew.'

'Why don't you speak to him?'

'He is no longer interested in what I have to say.'

'That's too bad.'

Swearingen's face was full, almost bloated. His eyes sagged. His head, almost bald, was pale in the lamplight. He pulled back the chair and sat and regretted the decision. He didn't like Ginevra standing over him.

'You've driven him away from me.'

'You give me too much credit. What I want to know is – do you really think Rayburn is such a bad influence on him?'

'You know he is.'

'No, my dear, I don't know. Andrew's just a young stallion. He can learn a thing or two from Rayburn.'

The furrows in her forehead grew deeper. Even in the lamplight – and he didn't like to admit it – she was still beautiful; perhaps not the beautiful, young brown-haired woman he had found singing in the chorus in New York. In those days she didn't wear silk, but now she made up for it. Only the finest – and only from Paris – that's what she wore, and that's what he paid for, and he never complained. So she stood there. She towered above him, in her dark blue silk dress that did not belong on a Wyoming ranch. He wanted to hear the voice of the land again, but it was gone. All he heard was her voice, and he considered that perhaps it was time to return to New York. Perhaps he would leave her here this time. He was certain he would not be lonely.

'Tell Rayburn to stay away from Andrew. If you insist on keeping Rayburn around, that's your business. But keep him away from Andrew.'

'I don't understand why you dislike Rayburn,' Swearingen said. 'After all, he comes from your neck of the woods. He's a good ole Missouri boy, born and raised. Just not one of the Johnny Reb variety. And, after the war, he helped clean things up. There was quite a bit of cleaning up to do. Maybe that's why you don't like him.'

'The man is evil.'

'Evil? That's a harsh word, Ginevra. You haven't been on the stage in a long time. There's no need to exaggerate. Rayburn gets things done. And I pay him – quite well, I might add – to get things done. Now I'll admit he's not perfect. He doesn't always do things the way I'd do them myself, but I believe Andrew can learn from him. In fact, Peter could also learn a thing or two from him. Today it's difficult to survive. And I'm not even talking about being successful. It's a hard world, Ginevra. Have you forgotten what it was like on a dirt farm? Have you forgotten what it was like being just a chorus singer in the theatre?'

'You've never let me forget it, and I suspect you never will. Richard, nothing good will come from Rayburn. Keep him away from Andrew.'

Swearingen thrust the chair behind him. He stood and clenched his fists. The violent move surprised her, and she stepped back.

'Ginevra, damn you. Don't – don't ever tell me what to do.'

He walked past her and went down the long dark hall to the door leading to the lower veranda. Rayburn was in the front yard beside the hitching post. He shook tobacco from a pouch into paper, rolled it, and struck a match. He returned the pouch to a small pocket in his black leather vest.

'There's been some trouble,' Rayburn said.

Ab Rayburn was thin – even the dark moustache was thin – and sometimes Swearingen wondered why a Wyoming wind scurrying across the grasslands didn't blow him away. His cheeks were hollow, and the eyes were sunken.

'Tell me about it,' Swearingen said.

'There was some business at the train we didn't count on,' Rayburn said.

'What kind of business?'

The foreman inhaled the smoke and released it.

'There was some shooting.'

'I didn't want any shooting.'

'It was a train robbery. Sometimes shots get fired.'

'Anybody killed?'

'Oh, yeah. Just four of the five men we hired.'

'What?'

'That's right,' Rayburn said. 'You heard me. I met with the one fellow who managed to ride away. He gave me the details. He was pretty shaken. I've seen corpses with more colour in their faces than he had.'

'You picked those men because you thought they were right for the job.'

'And they were. They were good with a gun, but no match for the man on the train they went up against.'

'Who was he?'

'I've asked around. I've been told his name is Ezra McPherson. I talked to this drummer. He said he saw it all. The passengers were lined up next to the train. One of the men hit a kid.'

'He did what?'

'He hit a kid, and this Ezra McPherson fellow didn't care for it. They exchanged a few words. Then the gun play started.'

Swearingen stared at the black outline of the mountains.

'These men you hired,' Swearingen said, 'they can't be traced to us. . . .'

'I rode up into the mining camps outside Deadwood and recruited them. They weren't any good as miners, obviously not any good as train robbers, just mostly down-on-their-luck drifters. They weren't known around here.'

'What about the man that got away?'

'He's long gone. I'm sure he's seen all of Wyoming that he cares to see. Mr Swearingen, if you wanted to scare those homesteaders, I'm sure you succeeded.'

'I wonder who this Ezra McPherson fellow is. He must be a

gunfighter. Ever heard of him?'

'I once knew of an Ezra McPherson. It was a long time ago. Probably not the same man.'

'It's not a common name. Was he a gunfighter?'

'Let's just say he was good with a gun. But like I said, it was a long time ago.'

'He must be a gunman. I just can't figure out why he would be on the train to Cheyenne. What do you make of it?'

'I've been told he was travelling with Luke Tisdale.'

'Luke Tisdale?'

'Yeah. He's come to pick up his brother and take him back East.'

'Luke Tisdale brought a gunman with him?'

'Looks that way. There was another fellow with them, but I don't know anything about him. I don't think he's a gunman. I think he's just a dude, maybe a friend of Tisdale's.'

Swearingen bowed his head and spat.

'Rayburn, this got a might careless, wouldn't you say? I've just spent a little time defending you to my wife. She doesn't appreciate your special talents, certainly not the way I do. And now I hear something like this. I'm not happy. I don't like being made unhappy. Do we understand each other?'

'We understand. I'm not happy either. Things will get sorted out.'

'I want you to send Curly into town. I want him to find Luke Tisdale. I want him to tell Tisdale his brother was working for me when he got killed. Invite him and the other two here for dinner tomorrow. I need to see them in person.'

'Yes, sir.'

The door opened and Peter Swearingen walked onto the veranda.

'And, Rayburn, I want you to find out something about this gunman. I want to know all about him – where he's from, who he works for, what he eats for breakfast. I want to know everything.'

Rayburn nodded and walked toward a small frame house not far from the bunkhouse. Peter came down the steps.

'What gunman? What's going on?'

'Nothing that concerns you,' Swearingen said.

Swearingen walked past his son and crossed the veranda and slammed the door behind him.

'And I hope you have a nice evening too,' Peter said.

Rayburn walked, barely visible, in the darkness and disappeared in his cabin. The heat still clung to the land. He didn't like the heat. It was even hard to take a good deep breath in it. Peter knew that Rayburn didn't care for him. He had heard him talk to some of the ranch hands.

'The man looks perpetually confused,' Rayburn said. 'He knows nothing about ranching. But I hear he's good with numbers. Lot of good it'll do him out here.'

Peter knew something was wrong. He had seen that look on his father's face too many times when things weren't going the way he had planned. He had once wished his father would talk, but he stopped wishing a long time ago. His father would talk to Andrew. He would tell him something about this gunman. Andrew was his favourite, and there was nothing Peter could do about it.

Anne Swearingen joined her husband on the porch. She reached up and touched his shoulder. He took her hand and held it tightly.

'What's wrong with your father?' she asked. 'I passed him in the hall. He didn't say a word.'

'He won't tell me. Whatever it is, it involves Rayburn.'

'There's an incredible coldness about Rayburn, even in this unforgiving heat. I don't like him.'

'Nor do I. Mother doesn't like him either. But Father has never been too concerned about what Mother and I like or dislike. It's been that way for years, and it isn't going to change.'

She stood close to him and they stared at the mountains at the edge of the darkened prairie.

'It's a beautiful country,' she said.

'It's a barren land. I prefer New York.'

'The baby will prefer Wyoming. He kicked a lot today. I think he was telling me he can't wait to set foot on this land.'

'So you know it's a "he".'

'The way he kicks – I'm sure of it.'

'I wish we were in New York. The medical care. . . .'

'Everything will be fine,' she said. 'You worry too much.'

He wrapped his arm around her. Laughter came from the bunkhouse. Peter knew the ranch hands shared Rayburn's opinion. They understood horses and pistols and rifles and the land. They didn't understand someone who made his living in the city. For that matter, they probably didn't understand Peter's father, but they understood his money and his power. For them, that was enough. Peter didn't offer those things. They liked his brother. Andrew just seemed to fit in. He had learned how to ride and how to shoot. He impressed them.

Rayburn walked out of his cabin, his cigarette a faint red in the darkness, and Peter watched. Rayburn went past the corral to the bunkhouse and stepped inside. A coyote suddenly cried.

'He sounds lonesome,' Anne said. 'You're not lonesome, are you?'

'No. Just hungry.'

Rayburn walked out of the bunkhouse. The coyote cried again. Laughter in the bunkhouse subsided. Rayburn thought back to his days in Missouri, days so long ago, days when the war would not die. In his mind the name turned over and over – Ezra McPherson.

CHAPTER 5

Piano music burst from the saloons. In the deepening twilight, Ezra, Luke and Marcus stood beneath a red-and-white-striped cloth overhang on the sidewalk and listened. Two cowboys galloped down the street. They jumped from their horses and tied the reins in front of the Two Rivers Saloon and hurried through the swinging doors. Shopkeepers emerged from their stores and locked the doors behind them. Luke scraped the sole of his shoe on the wooden sidewalk.

'The sheriff knows a lot more than he's telling,' Luke said. 'Marcus, you're a newspaperman. You know when people aren't being honest with you.'

'I've had some experience with that,' Marcus said.

'Then you agree?'

'I'm not sure, Luke. I wish I could tell you that the sheriff knows the whole story, but I can't. I'm really not sure.'

'Well, we're not settling anything just standing here,' Ezra said. 'When we were at the depot, I saw a hotel. It looked pretty nice. We need to get rooms.'

They walked up the street and came to the Cheyenne Hotel. It was three storeys, brick. They went into the small lobby and Luke rang the bell. The owner, a grey-haired black man, pushed past a blue curtain.

'Gentlemen, can I help you?'

'We want three rooms,' Luke said. 'I'm paying.'

'The newspaper will pay for mine,' Marcus said.

'Nonsense. Father wouldn't hear of it. Nor will I.'

'My name's Barclay,' the owner said. 'Where are you gents from?'

'From the East,' Luke said.

Luke wrote down the three names in the register.

'I have a special,' Barclay said. 'Five dollars per room per night.'

'Sounds like a good deal,' Luke said.

Barclay turned the register and looked at the names.

'Tisdale,' he said. 'You any kin to John Tisdale?'

'I'm his brother. I'm going to take him back East, back home.'

'I was awfully sorry to hear what happened. I met him only once or twice. He always seemed like a good gentleman. Always had real good manners. Such a shame nobody's been arrested.'

'I don't suppose you know what happened,' Luke said.

Barclay shook his head.

'No, I don't. You only hear things. I heard there was a poker game and then an argument. That's all I know.'

'Where can we get baths?' Ezra asked.

'Well, here, of course. There's a bath at the end of the hall. I bet you didn't expect us to have running water, now did you? Yes, sir, we have most of the conveniences you'd expect in a big city. Cheyenne just ain't what it used to be. Did you notice those electric street lamps? Have you ever seen such a thing? Well, we've got electric lights in our rooms. Yes, sir, we sure do. I know it takes some getting used to. We've come a long way.'

'Do you recommend a good restaurant?' Ezra said.

'Delmonico's. Two blocks up the street.'

'It has a good name,' Marcus said.

They took their keys and headed for the stairs.

'Gents, what I told you is the truth. We've come a long way. But there's still meanness. Your brother's death proves that. There are some people you'd best be wary of.'

'Thanks for the advice,' Ezra said.

They climbed the stairs to the second floor. Nothing fancy, Marcus saw, but the bed looked comfortable. After riding on the train, he welcomed the opportunity to sleep and not be moving at the same time. He walked to the window and raised it. More cowboys rode along the street. Suddenly he smiled. Two men rode bicycles and vanished into the night. The front wheels were high, and he wondered how the men kept their balance. Yes, things were not quite what he expected.

Marcus sat on the bed and closed his eyes. He saw the train robbers on the ground, blood soaking through their shirts and vests. Again he heard the screams of women and children. He wondered if he'd ever drive the sights and sounds of that day out of his mind. He opened his eyes and rubbed his temples. He would definitely have a story to write. Perhaps he would go on the lecture circuit and recount what he saw. People would pay to fill an opera house and listen. He was certain of that.

The hotel was quiet. He thought about Barclay's warning. Ezra didn't seem concerned, but Marcus didn't worry about him. He worried about Luke. His brother was dead and he wanted answers and no one wanted to talk about it. Harrison knew something. Luke was right about that. But Luke should not lose sight of the reason he was there. He should claim his brother's body and leave Cheyenne as quickly as possible. Marcus hadn't known Luke all that long, but he knew he was hardheaded.

There was a knock. The door was still open and Luke stood in the hall.

'Come on in,' Marcus said. 'Where's Ezra?'

'He's taking a bath. You can go next.'

'I'm not going to argue. My body is sore. I'm not sure it's ever going to feel quite right again.'

Luke sat in a straight chair and leaned against the wall. For a moment he stared at the ceiling. A light bulb dangled from a flimsy wire.

'I suppose I should turn that thing on,' Marcus said.

'I'm getting used to the darkness.'

'I don't think it's something you should ever get used to.'

The piano music grew louder. Marcus considered pulling down the window, but the heat was too intense.

'Marcus, do you have any brothers?'

'Yes. I had six. They rode with the cavalry in the war. I lost two at Shiloh. One was taken prisoner. He spent months at Rock Island. He got sick and just never recovered after he came back home. He died a few years ago.'

'I'm sorry.'

'In a way Ezra reminds me of him. The eyes. I'll never forget my brother's eyes, Luke. You looked into his eyes and knew he saw things he could never talk about, things that forever haunted him. I sense that it's like that with Ezra.'

'Ezra doesn't like to talk about the past.'

'We lived on a farm,' Marcus said. 'I was the youngest of the boys, too young to fight, though I sure wanted to. It was all men talked about – going off to fight. And everybody said it wouldn't last long. I still remember my brothers sitting astride their horses and waving good-bye. They looked so big. So big that nothing could ever hurt them. They rode past me and tipped their hats and smiled. I didn't let anybody see me cry. But after they left, I ran down to the creek, and I cried something fierce. One of the bird dogs went with me. He didn't know what was going on – first, my brothers leaving and, then, me crying. I didn't want them to go. Ma and Pa didn't want them to go either. But they went. When the four came back – and they didn't come back all at once – they weren't on horseback. They were walking. They were walking as if each step would be their last. I still don't know how they made it all the way home. They no longer looked big, and I could see they had been hurt. I look at Ezra and I see pretty much the same thing.'

'He's the closest thing to a friend I have,' Luke said. 'I wish I could say Father has been a friend to me. But he has a lot of responsibilities.'

'Your father is a powerful man.'

'That he is. The reason I became a doctor was that Father wanted me to be a doctor.'

'Perhaps he saw a talent in you that you didn't even realize you had.'

'Perhaps. It's as if he has a plan, and I'm part of the plan. I have to do things that are part of the plan. Here's an example. Marcus, there's a young lady in Boston – Ida Worthington – who comes from one of Boston's best families.'

'Let me guess. Your father wants you to marry her.'

'You guess correctly.'

'And you don't want to.'

'Ida is a wonderful girl. She's beautiful. She's bright. Most importantly, she has all the right social connections. Her family has deep roots in Boston. I respect her, but I don't love her. Father doesn't seem to think love has anything to do with it.'

'What will you do?'

'I'll tell you what I'm not going to do. I'm not going to marry her. Father won't be happy, but this is one time I'm going to tell him no. If John were here, he would agree with my decision.'

'Tell me about your brother,' Marcus said.

'He was older than me. Ten years older. He always looked out for me. He was kind. He always wanted to do the right thing. He was an excellent lawyer. He specialized in finance. As you might expect, his services were in great demand. In recent years I didn't see much of him. He travelled, and I was in medical school. I was hoping we'd be able to spend some time together later this year. I never imagined something like this would happen. Marcus, he was not a gambler. I don't believe a word the sheriff spoke.'

Shouts and laughter erupted from one of the saloons, and then quiet returned. Luke said nothing else. The door to the lobby opened and closed. Men spoke, but Marcus could not make out what they said. And then Barclay's voice was clear.

'That's my business, not yours.'

Then the door opened and closed again. Marcus looked at Luke. The young doctor still leaned back in the straight chair and stared at the ceiling. He apparently had not heard a thing.

CHAPTER 6

Jennifer Beauchamp sat on the bed in the small bedroom and looked down at her son. Even though it was hot, a sheet covered him to his shoulders. She stroked his hair. His breathing was soft. He slept soundly. No breeze came through the window, but it didn't matter. Her son was sleeping in a bed in a home, in a home where they had family. She rose and walked into the kitchen. Her sister, Charlotte, washed the dishes, and Silas dried them. Charlotte and Silas had lived in Cheyenne seven years. The years had been hard. Charlotte never complained, but Jennifer knew. Her sister's face had aged. The exuberance in her eyes had faded. Silas still looked the same – still heavyset, still red-faced. He still wore red galluses – 'I expect to be buried in them,' he had once said – over a white shirt.

'Is the boy asleep?' Silas asked.

'He wasn't in bed a minute before his eyes closed.'

Charlotte looked at the bedroom door, and Jennifer knew how much her sister had wanted a family. A year after she and Silas came to Cheyenne, she gave birth. The baby lived only a week. There had been no other children.

'There's still some coffee,' Charlotte said.

'Yes, thank you.'

'I'll take care of it,' Silas said. 'You sit down and rest. You've

41

had quite a day.'

She sat at the small pine table and Silas took chipped Blue Willow cups to the wood-burning stove and poured the coffee. Charlotte left the dishpan and joined them in the dim light of the lamp that flickered in the middle of the table.

'I can't tell you how grateful I am. . . .'

'There's no need to thank us,' Charlotte said.

'Besides, this town needs more schoolteachers,' Silas said. 'More people keep moving here. That means more children. We need more schoolteachers.'

'Silas likes to talk about more people coming here,' Charlotte said. 'It means more schoolteachers. That's true. But it also means more customers in the store. That's what you're really interested in, isn't it, dear?'

'I make no apologies. When more people come to Cheyenne, business grows. In fact, I may have to open a store in Laramie. Charlotte, don't look so surprised. I've given a lot of thought to it. You ladies don't mind if I light up my pipe?'

'Go ahead,' his wife said.

'I'm glad your store is doing so well,' Jennifer said.

'Moving out here was a good decision. I was never cut out to be a farmer, and things were just too tough in South Carolina. I wasn't sure any store I opened in Charleston would be accepted. I didn't have any kind of pedigree. Out here no one cares about your pedigree.'

Charlotte looked at her sister and rolled her eyes.

'Silas has made that store his life. Today, after he brought us home from the depot, he went back to it. His employees could have closed, but he has to have his hand in everything.'

'You make it sound like I don't trust my employees. I just like to oversee things, that's all.'

'Sometimes I think Franklin should have opened a store,' Jennifer said. 'I think he would have been successful.'

'Franklin was a fine man,' Charlotte said.

'I always thought a lot of him,' Silas said. 'I hated to hear about his passing. I'm sure it was hard on Bobby.'

The sweet aroma of the pipe smoke reminded Jennifer of years past, sitting in the swing on the front porch, Franklin Beauchamp sitting in the rocker, peaceful with his pipe at the end of the day.

'Bobby is incredibly resilient. It's been hard, but he has managed.'

'The gentleman at the depot seemed to take an interest in you,' Charlotte said.

'He and his friends were just fellow travellers.'

'I'd say one of his friends was more than just a traveller,' Silas said. 'At the store this evening the only thing folks talked about was the train robbery.'

Steam lingered above her cup, and she remembered.

'Everything happened so quickly. This man – he was awful – he hit Bobby. And then there was gunfire. And then it was over. These men lay on the ground, dead. That's a sight I won't soon forget.'

'I'm sorry you and Bobby had to see something like that,' Charlotte said. 'Wyoming has changed so much in recent years. Oh, you still hear about desperadoes. They're not all gone, not by any stretch of the imagination. But things have changed – for the better. Train robberies and gunfights live mostly in the dime novels. At least that's what I like to believe.'

Silas stared at his wife.

'Why are you looking like that?' Charlotte asked. 'You agree, don't you? We have changed.'

'Yes, we have changed.'

'Well, try to sound like you mean it.'

'Charlotte, you know as well as I do there may be trouble.'

'Trouble?' Jennifer asked. 'What kind of trouble?'

'Let's not talk about it,' Charlotte said.

'No, I think she should know.'

'Know what?' Jennifer asked.

'Many of the people coming here are homesteaders,' Silas said. 'Most of the people on the train today were homesteaders. They've bought land and they intend to farm it. And there's nothing wrong with that. It's all perfectly legal.'

'Then why is there trouble?'

'Some men in this state, especially around Cheyenne, think their cattle should graze all over the prairie. That's the way it's always been. If their herds mingle, then the ranch hands just separate them periodically. You can say there's honour among them. They keep the cattle that's theirs. They don't take from their neighbours. They see the homesteaders as a threat to their way of life. The homesteaders put up fences. The range becomes closed. One thing you have to understand is that these big ranchers are wealthy. Many have come from the East and invested in the cattle industry. They consider themselves gentlemen. They've even built an impressive gentlemen's club downtown. But, you know, to get their way, they don't care if they're gentlemen. They don't like being told what they can and cannot do. Their investments have suffered in recent years. We've had some brutal winters, followed by some brutal hot, dry summers. The herds need more and more grass. Too many of their cows have been lost. The arrival of homesteaders means there won't be as much pasture. Like I said, it means trouble.'

'I think a more pleasant subject is in order,' Charlotte said. 'Let's talk about the man you were with at the depot. I believe you said he's a doctor.'

'Yes.'

'What's his name?' Silas asked.

'Tisdale.'

'Oh, damn.'

'Silas, watch your language.'

'He's got to be related to John Tisdale.'

'We don't know that.'

'Well, I bet he is.'

'Who's John Tisdale?' Jennifer asked.

'A man who was killed awhile back. He was a lawyer, a good one I've been told. He worked for Richard Swearingen, one of the cattlemen. I heard the undertaker was holding the body for somebody to take it back East. I guess that's what that young fellow has come to do. The man who did all the fancy shooting – was he with Tisdale?'

'Yes.'

Silas bit down on the pipe, but it seemed to give him no pleasure. He sat in silence. Jennifer finished her coffee and walked onto the front porch. It was small, smaller than what she and her husband had had in Charleston. The house was on the outskirts of town, beyond the mansions. A white picket fence went around the front yard. It was a comfortable house, but she knew she would have to find a place of her own. She and her son could not stay in the house indefinitely.

She sat in the swing and felt Franklin sitting beside her. She felt the warmth of his touch. She turned and saw emptiness. For a moment she thought she was going to cry. She struggled. She must not let herself cry. She thought then about the young doctor. He was concerned about her son. Bobby liked him. She could tell. And she thought about the man who had put an abrupt end to the train robbery. He had cared about her son too.

CHAPTER 7

The dining room of Delmonico's was large with floor-to-ceiling windows across the front. Murmurs of conversation and the clatter of white china greeted Ezra, Luke and Marcus at the door. A white-bearded man in a dark suit approached. To Marcus, the man's accent sounded British.

'Dinner, gentlemen?'

'Yes,' Ezra said.

'Please follow me.'

They sat at a table in the far corner of the room. Ezra took the chair next to the wall. Conversation at the other tables subsided. Marcus realized they were being watched.

'Let 'em look,' Ezra said. 'Once they get their eyes full, they'll go about their business, which should be eating.'

Each table had a small lamp in the middle.

'It's kind of dark in here,' Luke said. 'I've always thought that the fancier a restaurant is, the darker it is.'

The diners stared at the three men but then looked away and slowly resumed their conversations. A young woman in a white apron came out of the kitchen and walked up to their table. Her face was red from the heat of the kitchen.

'Velcome to Delmonico's,' she said.

'The food smells awfully good,' Luke said.

'Ve have good food.'

'Where are you from?' Marcus asked.

'My family come from Germany. Ve vork the land. My ma and pa vork hard. I come to the city and vork in Delmonico's. Ve have good steak. You want steak?'

'Steak sounds good,' Luke said.

'Vhat you drink? Ve have good coffee. Best in Cheyenne.'

'Coffee will be fine,' Luke said.

Occasionally diners glanced at them. All it took was one look into Ezra's dark eyes, and then they lowered their heads. The patrons were well-dressed – suits, ties. The women wore long fine silk dresses. Ezra looked at the men and the women and thought about a West that was different. In those days there wasn't a whole lot of silk. There weren't too many restaurants like this one. But just when he thought the West had changed, he remembered the train, the robbery, the Colt .45 in his hand blazing, men lying dead in the dust that grew red in the hot August sun.

'Ezra, did you grow up in the West?' Marcus asked.

Ezra hesitated.

'Yes, I grew up in the West,' he said.

'Where?'

'Stokesbury, why is it I always get the feeling you're doing an interview?'

'It's my job.'

Ezra removed his hat and set it on the floor next to his chair. In the dim lamplight his hair shone grey. It was thinning on top.

'I've travelled a great deal. It doesn't really matter where I grew up. It was so long ago anyway.'

'Ezra taught me how to hunt quail,' Luke said. 'On Jekyll Island. He taught me how the dogs work, how to flush a covey. Ezra knows everything about hunting.'

'You caught on quickly,' Ezra said. 'Stokesbury, do you do any hunting?'

47

'I grew up on a farm. I used to hunt. We had some wonderful bird dogs. But I live in the city now. I hunt stories for the newspaper.'

The young lady from Germany juggled three white china platters in her hands and set them on the table. A young boy, younger than she, brought coffee. He said nothing. He only nodded when spoken to. The dark crusted steaks sizzled next to golden biscuits.

The three men tucked their white cloth napkins into their shirt collars and cut into the red in their steaks and ate. The girl remained beside the table to receive the verdict.

'Splendid,' Luke said. 'I believe I speak for the three of us. Some of the best beef we've had.'

The girl smiled and hurried back into the kitchen.

'I must say Cheyenne exceeds all my expectations,' Marcus said.

'Don't be fooled by appearances,' Ezra said.

During the meal they talked little. After he finished his steak, Ezra lifted the cup of coffee. Before he sipped, he saw the woman. She stood just inside the door and talked with the same man who had greeted them. She was tall and slim, with dark brown hair tucked beneath a purple hat that matched her long purple silk dress. Lace wrapped around her wrists. The man pointed to their table, and she walked toward them.

'You must be this famous gunman I keep hearing about,' she said.

Ezra lowered the cup.

'I wouldn't say I'm a gunman. I wouldn't say I'm famous.'

'Your first quote. And that's a pretty good one, I must say.'

She slid a chair from a vacant table next to theirs and sat. She reached into her purse and withdrew a small tablet and pencil.

'If you don't mind my asking,' Ezra said, 'just who are you?'

'Eloise Endicott. I'm the editor and publisher of the

Cheyenne Daily Times.'

Luke shifted uncomfortably in his chair. Ezra appeared incredulous. Her eyes did not shrink from his.

'You look surprised. Don't you think it's appropriate for a woman to run a newspaper?'

'It's not really any of my business.'

'What is your business, Mr McPherson? That is your name, I believe – Ezra McPherson.'

'I don't believe Mr McPherson is interested in an interview,' Luke said.

'And who are you?'

'My name is Luke Tisdale.'

She stopped writing.

'Tisdale?'

'Yes, ma'am. Ezra and I are from Jekyll Island, off the coast of Georgia.'

'Are you any relation to John Tisdale?'

'He was my brother.'

'I see,' she said, and she lay the notepad in her lap.

'Did you know him?'

'No, not really. I knew who he was when I saw him on the street.'

'Since you run the newspaper, you must know what happened.'

'I only know he was shot and killed,' she said. 'Why don't you stop by the newspaper office tonight? You can read the article. We work late.'

'Yes, I think I will. Thank you.'

'The office is at the end of the street. And you, Mr McPherson, are you the hired gun Mr Tisdale has brought to set things right in this town?'

'I'm not a hired gun,' Ezra said. 'Do things need to be set right in Cheyenne?'

'If you stay here long enough, you'll find out. And you,'

49

she said, and she turned toward Marcus. 'I don't mean any offence, but you don't look like a hired gun.'

'No. The pen is mightier than the hired gun. My name is Marcus Stokesbury. I'm a newspaperman. I work in Atlanta.'

'You don't say. A fellow journalist. You three gentlemen are an interesting lot. I want all of you to come by the newspaper tonight. Mr Stokesbury, you may be surprised at our operation. Mr McPherson, perhaps you will be inclined to sit for an interview.'

A man in leather chaps entered the room. He stopped briefly and surveyed the room and ignored the white-bearded man. The jingle of spurs followed him across the floor. His face was long, deeply-tanned. He looked to his left and right, as if someone might object to his being in Delmonico's. He walked to their table and removed his hat. Strands of thin, wet hair clung to the side of his head.

'Curly, you look like you've been trying to outride a storm,' Eloise said.

He looked at the rug and expected to see dust that had fallen from his chaps. He raised his head and focused on Ezra.

'I asked around. Folks said you were in here. Are you Tisdale?'

Ezra nodded toward Luke.

'I'm Curly Pike. I work for Mr Swearingen. Your brother was an employee. Mr Swearingen said to tell you he'd like to meet you and your friends. Tomorrow at dinner.'

'Certainly. I'd like to meet him.'

'You staying at Barclay's hotel? I'll bring a wagon by there around ten.'

'Ezra, we need to go to Slade's,' Luke said.

'We'll do it early.'

'Curly, is the publisher of the town's newspaper also invited?'

The ranch hand didn't know what to say. He hadn't expected Eloise Endicott to be in the restaurant. He had received no instructions for such an eventuality. She was a lady. How could he say no to a lady? What would Swearingen say when he found out she would be coming?

'I reckon so, ma'am,' Curly said. 'I'll pick you up first.'

'See that you do. I'll be at the newspaper.'

'Good night, folks.'

As a boy, Curly had learned to back away from danger, not simply to turn. And so he backed away, as if danger lurked at the table. He closed the door and went into the night.

'Richard Swearingen is pretty much a king in Wyoming,' she said. 'You boys need to be on your best behaviour.'

'Who is this Swearingen fellow?' Ezra asked.

'He made his money as a financier in New York. Mr Tisdale, I believe your father has done quite well in steel.'

'And in railroads.'

'I suspect he knows Swearingen. A few years ago Swearingen came to Wyoming and started buying land, a lot of land. Today he has one of the biggest ranches anywhere close to Cheyenne. But he's not alone. He and the other cattlemen don't want fences. If his cattle graze on someone else's land, then so be it. The cattlemen don't see eye to eye with the new homesteaders.'

'Has there been trouble?' Ezra asked.

'Yes.'

'Was my brother involved?' Luke asked.

'I don't know what your brother was involved in. I was told he handled Swearingen's legal interests. Swearingen has his family here. I'm sure you'll meet them tomorrow. He has two sons, Peter and Andrew. His wife, Ginevra. . . .'

'Ginevra?' Ezra said.

'Yes. Ginevra.'

Ezra's fingers tightened around the coffee cup, and

Marcus saw.

'I believe she's from Missouri,' Eloise said. 'Perhaps you once knew her.'

'Why would I have known her?'

'I've travelled a great deal, and I'm pretty accurate when it comes to identifying an accent, Mr McPherson. You may come from Georgia, but you're not originally from Georgia. Mr Stokesbury, of course, is. But you, Mr McPherson, your accent is a bit flatter – Missouri, Kansas maybe. But I'd lay odds on Missouri.'

'You should be careful how you bet your money,' Ezra said.

'I am, Mr McPherson, I am. Anyway, when you meet the Swearingens, I think you'll like the oldest son, Peter. He's married, and they're about to have a baby. The younger son, Andrew, is a hothead, not anything like his brother. If he's not careful, he's going to end up in some kind of trouble. Well, I'd best be going. Please, don't stand. Keep your seats.'

Ezra watched her until she was gone.

'She invited herself to dinner,' Marcus said. 'Imagine that.'

'She's the new woman,' Luke said.

'What?' Ezra asked.

'The new woman. I've read about them. They're independent. Ezra, I think she likes you.'

'She wants an interview.'

'No, she likes you. But as far as the interview goes, I don't think it's such a good thing. You're not going to consent to it, are you?'

'No.'

'If you give anyone an interview, it needs to be me,' Marcus said.

Luke paid the German girl for their suppers, and the three men walked outside. Ezra stood at the edge of the sidewalk and listened. The piano music was the same as it was in other towns, other saloons, other days.

Across the street a slender figure stood in darkness. They saw him.

'It looks like the deputy,' Luke said.

'He's just trying to be a lawman,' Ezra said.

They walked back to the hotel. Marcus thought that the night would bring some measure of coolness, but he was wrong. The heat had settled and didn't want to leave.

Barclay stood behind his desk, and Marcus thought the old man looked worried. They climbed the stairs and each went to his room. Ezra opened the door and stepped inside.

Before he shut the door, the hammer of a pistol clicked. He did not see the pistol, but he knew the mouth of the barrel was only inches from his head.

'I'd recognize the click of that Schofield anywhere,' Ezra said.

'I told you what I'd do if you ever came west of the Mississippi again. I said I'd kill you. Remember?'

'Yeah. It's kind of hard to forget something like that.'

'But you know what?'

'What?'

'I'm just not in much of a mood to do any killing.'

The man released the hammer and he and Ezra laughed. Marcus was in his room. He heard the commotion. He had never heard Ezra laugh, so at first he wasn't sure who it was. Luke hurried to Ezra's door.

'Ezra, is everything all right?'

Ezra pulled the chain at the light bulb, and suddenly shadows of the men flickered on the wall.

'You boys come in,' Ezra's visitor said, and he removed his bowler and hung it on the back of a straight chair. 'Ezra and I are old friends.'

'This is Owen Chesterfield,' Ezra said. 'His name is a bit highfalutin, but that's the only thing highfalutin about him.'

It was obvious to Marcus that Owen Chesterfield hadn't

backed away from too many meals. His head was bald. The skin was pulled tight across his forehead.

'Gentlemen. Let's see – you must be young Luke Tisdale, and you must be Marcus Stokesbury.'

'How, may I ask, do you know who we are?' Marcus said.

Owen looked at Ezra and winked.

'I'm paid to know all sorts of things,' Owen said. 'I need a drink. Travelling makes a man thirsty. I got into town just a little while ago. Ezra, you got anything decent to drink around here?'

'Do I look like I run a saloon?'

'You look like you belong in a saloon. Let's go find one.'

'We just had supper,' Luke said.

'It's best to drink on a full stomach, young man,' Owen said. 'You're a doctor. You should know that. It's a proven scientific fact. Come on. Let's just follow the piano music. I'm buying.'

CHAPTER 8

Curly stood across the street from the Two Rivers Saloon. He had considered O'Faolin's, but it had too many memories, some he preferred to forget. Dim, smoke-crusted light spilled through the narrow windows of the Two Rivers onto the sidewalk. He needed to get back to the ranch, but he needed a drink more. He could still see Ezra McPherson's eyes. He didn't like him. He had the look of death about him.

Rayburn had called Curly out of the bunkhouse. He gave him his assignment. Curly was hot. He was tired. Riding into town was just not something he cared to do, but he knew better than to protest. When Rayburn wanted you to do something, you did it. You didn't complain. But Curly noticed something he thought interesting. Rayburn was nervous. He had never seen Rayburn nervous before. Rayburn mentioned the train robbery. He tossed out the name McPherson, someone Curly had never heard of. But it was someone Rayburn apparently once had known, probably someone he thought he would never see again. Now that Curly had met McPherson, he understood why Rayburn would be nervous.

Curly crossed the street and hurried through the swinging

doors. Upstairs, at the red-draped window, Andrew Swearingen stood and watched. What was Curly doing in town? He wondered if his ma had sent him to fetch her youngest boy home. She was always concerned about his whereabouts.

'Why don't you come back to bed, honey?'

Andrew turned and finished buttoning his shirt.

'I got things to do,' he said.

'Better than this, honey?'

She lay on her side beneath the white sheet and drew a deep puff from her cigarette.

'Would I get a discount?' he asked.

'Well, now, honey, that hurts my feelings. You must think all I'm interested in is your money.'

He buckled his gun belt and tied down the holster. In the lamplight his face was pale – she figured that no matter how much time he spent in the sun, he would always look pale – and she realized how young he really was. He was just a boy. She remembered what Rayburn had told her: 'He needs breaking in.'

'When are you going to take me to the gentlemen's club?' she asked.

'They call it a gentlemen's club for a reason.'

'If they built a ladies' club, I'd let you escort me.'

'If they built a ladies' club, do you think they'd let you in?'

'You go to hell, Andrew Swearingen,' she said, and she mashed the end of the cigarette into a saucer on the table next to the bed.

'That's where I'm heading, Rose. But I'll have plenty of company.'

She propped herself on her elbow and watched him. He lifted his wide-brimmed hat and started for the door. Downstairs the piano player was putting everything he had into 'The Yellow Rose of Texas'.

'Am I your yellow rose of Texas?'

He wanted to say faded rose, but he thought better of it.

'I'm not partial to roses.'

'But you're partial to me.'

'Yeah, sure.'

'Tell me something, Andrew. Do your folks know what you do when you come to town?'

'That's not any of your concern. You just do what I pay you to do, and everything will be just fine.'

He stood at the door and surveyed the red room – red drapes, red upholstery, red coverlet that lay on the floor. Rayburn had introduced him to Rose – 'not a spring chicken,' he had said, 'but she'll do for now.' He stared at her.

'I don't like it when you just stand and stare,' she said.

'Why?'

'It's like you don't approve of what you see. It's like you're some big-shot from the East who thinks he's too good for me.'

Her shoulders were large, bare. Her cheeks were puffed, as if she had been stung by bees. Her eyes were small, almost lost in the fullness of the face.

'Maybe I am too good for you, Rose. Did that ever occur to you?'

'You know what, honey?' she said. 'You may be too good for me, but you'll never be as tall as me. That's the way it is when you're the runt of the litter.'

She laughed and sat up, and he walked to the edge of the bed and looked down at her. The slap was fast, like the strike of a rattler, and loud. She shrieked and her head flew back against the wrought iron headboard. She reached up and touched her mouth. Blood trickled down her chin.

'You bastard! You no-good, puny bastard!'

He laughed and left the room.

Ezra and Owen Chesterfield went through the swinging doors

first. Marcus and Luke followed. Men, some dressed in suits, some dressed in jeans and cotton work shirts still bearing dust from the trail into town, clustered around the tables. They talked and laughed and smoke and drank, and some pondered the hand they had been dealt. All turned and saw the four men come into the saloon. Heavy cigar and cigarette smoke hung in the room. The piano music, once loud and raucous, slowed its tempo. The piano player, gaunt as if he suffered from consumption, looked nervously over his shoulder. His long, crooked fingers hit the wrong keys. Curly sat at one of the wooden tables and lowered his head. He didn't want Ezra to notice him.

'Curly Pike, you're out a bit late for a ranch hand,' Ezra said.

'Bartender, you got any good Kentucky bourbon?' Owen asked.

The bartender wiped his hands on his soiled apron.

'I certainly do.'

'Then four glasses and a bottle.'

'Coming right up.'

The bartender set four glasses on the bar and poured and set the bottle down. The man was a friendly sort, Marcus observed. His dark beard was neatly trimmed. Even while he poured the drinks, his eyes surveyed the saloon, as if concerned trouble might erupt at any moment. Everyone seemed to be enjoying himself. Not much chance of trouble.

'Ezra, it's been a long time since we shared a drink,' Owen said.

'We never shared a drink.'

'You may be right. Here's to the drink we never shared but should have and which we will now make up for.'

Owen and Ezra touched glasses and drank. Owen coughed.

'Luke, you and Marcus go easy on it. That's some powerful

bourbon, not quite as smooth as the Kentucky I'm used to.'

Luke and Marcus just stared at the glasses before them. Neither was in a hurry to pick them up.

'Owen, what brings you to Cheyenne?' Ezra asked.

'Mr Tisdale sent me a telegram.'

'You know my father?' Luke asked.

'Indeed I do, son. Your father and I have known each other for many years. He said Ezra was going to look after you, and he wanted me to look after Ezra.'

'I don't need looking after,' Ezra said.

'After that fancy gunplay earlier today, I'd say you need looking after.'

'So you've heard.'

'Hell, Ezra, I'm sure folks as far away as Arizona have heard by now. And they're all wondering, "Who is this Ezra McPherson fellow?" '

Owen poured himself and Ezra another glass.

'Are you the man who stopped the train robbery?' the bartender asked.

'You're looking at him,' Owen said. 'He's a bit shy. He doesn't like to talk about his accomplishments.'

'I don't think Mr Tisdale sent you here to get on my nerves,' Ezra said.

'Mister, that must have been really something,' the bartender said. 'I wish I could've seen it.'

'There wasn't much to see,' Ezra said.

'Mr Chesterfield, what is your connection to Mr Tisdale?' Marcus asked. 'What's more – I'd really like to know what your connection to Ezra is.'

'I bet you would.'

'Stokesbury is working on a story,' Ezra said.

'Mysteries reveal themselves in due time,' Owen said. 'And then, sometimes, not at all.'

A large man pushed through the swinging doors and

stopped. He pushed his hat back on his head and looked at each table. He then came up to the bar. Ezra saw him in the mirror behind the bar and decided he was a farmer. He just had that look about him. Deeply tanned face, large hands made rugged from gripping plough handles. He wore a flannel shirt even in the unbearable heat. The hair sticking out beneath the hat was the colour of wheat in the midst of a drought.

'Dooley, where is she?' the farmer asked.

'Sven, I'll be with you in a minute.'

'Dooley, where is she?'

The bartender, perplexed, dried a glass and set it on the counter beneath the mirror.

'Sven, it's getting late. Why don't you go on home?'

'I want to see Rose.'

The bartender was annoyed. He leaned over the bar and whispered.

'She's busy upstairs. Do I have to draw you a picture?'

Ezra observed the man. He had a pistol tucked into his belt, no holster.

'Son, is there some kind of trouble?' Owen asked.

'It's none of your affair, old man.'

Owen raised both hands.

'Don't get upset, son. I'm just trying to help.'

'I don't want your help.'

'Let him be,' Ezra said. 'He's got an old navy revolver in his belt.'

'I know he's got an old navy revolver in his belt. Do you think I've gone blind in my old age?'

Andrew Swearingen stood on the balcony at the top of the stairs. He studied the men at the bar. He didn't recognize four of them. And there was Sven, lovesick Sven, homesteader in love with Rose. Andrew went down the stairs and stopped on the landing. Rose was above him, clutching a robe. Her chin was covered with blood.

'You'll burn in hell, Andrew Swearingen! You'll burn in hell!'

Andrew did not answer. He went on down the stairs and stopped at Curly's table.

'Curly, what are you doing here?'

'Just having a drink.'

'You mean you're not looking for me?'

'No. Why should I be looking for you?'

Andrew took two steps toward the door but stopped. The farmer stood in front of him.

'You hurt Rose.'

'No, farm boy, I did not hurt Rose.'

'Then why is there blood all over her face?'

'She drinks too much. She stumbled and fell down on her face. She needs to do something about that heavy drinking.'

'You hurt her.'

'Sven, come back here and have a drink,' the bartender said. 'It's on the house. I don't want no trouble.'

'Listen to the barkeep,' Owen said. 'No point in someone getting hurt over a woman.'

'Shut up, old man,' Sven said.

The men playing poker and smoking no longer talked. They no longer laughed. The piano player jumped from the bench and went into the back room. Sven's right hand rested on the handle of his pistol. Ezra wondered about the old navy revolver. It probably hadn't been fired in years.

'Farm boy, go back to where you came from,' Andrew said.

'Andrew Swearingen, you're rich. Your daddy's rich. You think you can run all over people – just because you've got money. I aim to prove you can't.'

'Well, quit talking. You got proving to do? Go ahead.'

Sven grasped his pistol and pulled it free from the belt. After the loud gunshot, pain ripped through his abdomen and out his back. He grimaced and dropped to his knees. His pistol hit the floor. He clutched his stomach with both hands and fell over.

Luke hurried to his side.

'Somebody give me a towel.'

The bartender threw him a towel. It was dirty but better than nothing. Luke folded the towel and pressed it against the wound. The big man groaned. Andrew still held his revolver, but his hand shook. Surprise shone in his eyes. He had just shot a man, and the man now lay dying in the dust on the floor.

'You can put that thing up now,' Owen said. 'You've done enough damage with it.'

The farmer rolled back and forth on the floor and wept. Rose ran downstairs and stopped at the man's feet. Upstairs more women in robes stood at the bannister. A few men stood beside them and smoked cigarettes and stared nonchalantly at the scene below.

'We need to get him to the doctor's office,' Luke said.

The farmer's legs shook for a few moments and then grew rigid. His hands dropped from the wound. Luke checked his pulse and stood.

'Maybe not the doctor's office,' Owen said.

'Maybe not,' Luke said.

Deputy Stuart walked into the saloon and saw the farmer. Stunned, he looked at Ezra.

'Have you killed another man?' Stuart asked.

'Not so fast, sonny,' Owen said. 'That young buck there with the dazed look on his face is the one who's given the undertaker some business.'

Stuart turned toward the bartender.

'The fellow's right,' Dooley said. 'Sven pulled his pistol. Swearingen shot in self-defence.'

Ezra set his glass down. He wanted to get out of the saloon.

He had seen too much self-defence. The farmer never had a chance. He remembered what Eloise had said about the younger Swearingen brother. Now he had shot and killed – probably his first man. He had probably practised in a pasture. He had probably shot at tin cans and whiskey bottles that couldn't shoot back. And he had probably wondered what it would be like to face a man. He had wondered what it would be like to draw faster and fire faster. Ezra suspected what he was feeling now – not anything like what he had imagined. Somebody had taught Andrew Swearingen how to shoot. But nobody had told him how he would feel after killing a man.

Her large shoulders sagging, Rose turned and walked past Andrew. She did not look up. She climbed the stairs. By the time she reached the top, the others along the bannister had returned to their rooms. Curly walked up to Andrew.

'We'd better get out of here,' Curly said.

Andrew hardly heard him. It was as if the voice came from deep within a cistern. Everything seemed hollow. He and Curly walked outside to their horses. Before he lifted his boot into the stirrup, he bent over and vomited. Hearing the sound and smelling the smell, Curly felt sick too. He gripped the saddle horn and wondered what the old man would have to say about all this. He wondered what the old man's wife would have to say, but somehow he knew.

'He didn't leave me any choice,' Andrew said, and he heaved himself up into the saddle. 'I didn't want to kill him. You believe me, don't you, Curly?'

'Sure I believe you,' Curly said, and he didn't know what to believe except that a man lay dead on the floor of the saloon.

Andrew and Curly spurred their horses and headed down the street, past darkened storefronts. Andrew felt as if in the blackness hundreds of eyes peered out at him. He heard whispers upon the wind, 'He's now a killer.'

Stuart walked over to the farmer and motioned toward two men who had vacated their chairs.

'You men haul him over to Slade's,' the deputy said.

'Slade turns in early,' one said.

'Then wake him up.'

The two men considered running out the door, but they liked Cheyenne. They liked the saloon. They did as they were told.

Stuart walked to the bar next to Owen.

'And who are you?'

Owen reached into his jacket pocket and withdrew a small card.

'Pinkerton,' Stuart said. 'What's a Pinkerton doing in Cheyenne?'

'Just taking in the sights,' Owen said. 'And apparently there are plenty to take in.'

Stuart turned toward the spot on the floor where the farmer had lain. A pool of blood shone a dull red.

'This sort of thing just doesn't happen around here,' Stuart said. 'Dooley, the sheriff isn't going to like this.'

'What was I supposed to do? Sven was determined to fight. If I'd gotten in the middle of it, I would have been the one shot.'

Stuart faced Ezra.

'And there was nothing you could do?'

'No, Deputy, there was nothing I could do.'

Stuart again looked at the pool of blood and walked out.

'Young man, you can wash your hands out back,' the bartender said.

Luke held his reddened hands before him. Suddenly he felt useless. He was a doctor and he was unable to help.

'Go on, Luke,' Ezra said.

Marcus lowered his head. He didn't want to see any more dead men. Shoot-outs in dime novels came back to him, but they were not like what he had just seen. Fingers and feet twitching. White faces covered with the sweat of death. He looked at Ezra. Nothing seemed to bother him. He wanted to remember the impassive look on Ezra's face. One day he would describe it in words. Ezra must have seen this sort of thing before, perhaps many times before.

'Stokesbury, are you all right?' Ezra asked.

'Yeah, sure, I'm all right,' Marcus said.

'Stokesbury is a newspaper reporter,' Owen said. 'He can handle things like this. Isn't that right, Stokesbury?'

Some of the patrons returned to their tables and sat, but some collected their winnings and left. Those that stayed studied their cards and waited for the piano music, but it did not come. The piano player did not return.

'We haven't had trouble like this in a long time,' the bartender said. 'The deputy was right. Sheriff Harrison won't like hearing about this. He'll march in here and threaten to close me down.'

'It wasn't your fault,' Owen said.

'I've never cared for Andrew Swearingen,' Dooley said. 'He's always reminded me of a rattlesnake. Mister, I hope you don't mind me saying, but you look awful familiar.'

'I doubt you've seen me before,' Ezra said.

'No, no, I'm sure I have – at least pretty sure. What about Dodge City? Ever been to Dodge?'

'Maybe. I've been lots of places.'

'Come to think of it, it might not have been Dodge. Some place in Missouri.'

'No point in rehashing what's done,' Owen said. 'There's no future in the past.'

Luke returned to the bar but did not touch the glass before him. He wondered whether anyone had been with his brother during those last moments to offer a word of comfort. He wondered whether John had died alone.

'Drink up, young man,' Owen said. 'It'll make you feel better.'

'I want to walk over to the newspaper office. I want to read the article about my brother.'

CHAPTER 9

Andrew slid down from his mare and slowly walked up the steps of the house. Once on the porch, he stood still. He listened. He heard no sounds from within. Perhaps his mother was asleep. He had noticed riding up that all the windows were dark. But sometimes she would sit in a room in darkness, alone. He knew. He had seen her. He turned toward Curly.

'You mind taking care of my horse?'

'I don't mind.'

Andrew walked into the darkness of the entrance hall, and Curly took the reins and walked their horses toward the barn. Near the gate of the pasture Rayburn stepped in his way. Curly had not seen him. Suddenly he was there.

'Where've you been?'

The voice was low, hoarse. Curly would know Rayburn's voice at any time of day or night.

'In town. There's been trouble.'

'What kind of trouble?'

'Andrew shot a man.'

'Shot a man? Who?'

'Sven, that big farmer from west of town.'

'Andrew didn't kill him, did he?'

'Hell yeah, he killed him. Shot him in the gut and must have hit something pretty important. Rayburn, you taught him how to shoot real good. He's fast. No question about that. I had no idea somebody from New York could be that fast. But young Sven wasn't much to compete against. Just a ploughboy. And now he's a dead ploughboy.'

'Was it self-defence?'

'Clear self-defence. Witnesses and everything. Even that man who stopped the train robbery was there. Him and Luke Tisdale and the other dude – they were all there, and some fellow I didn't recognize.'

'What about the dinner invite? Did you do what you were supposed to do?'

'Yes, I delivered the invite. They're coming. And so is Miss Endicott, the newspaper woman.'

'Nobody invited her.'

'She invited herself.'

'Swearingen will love that bit of news. Tell me – what did you think of McPherson?'

Rayburn was still nervous. Curly sensed it.

'I can't say I like being around him. Why do you ask?'

'Just curious.'

'Do you know him?'

'No, I don't know him. Why should I?'

Andrew closed the door as quietly as he could, but it squeaked. He put his hat on the hall-tree and started down the hall. His mother rose from a chair and stood at the foot of the stairs. He could not see her face in the darkness.

'Have you been to town?' she asked.

'Yes.'

'It's awfully late.'

'I know.'

He wanted to brush past her, but he thought better of it.

'What whore were you with tonight?'

'I'm not going to answer a question like that.'

She slapped his face. It was a hard, ringing slap, and he reached up and touched the redness.

'You'll answer any question I ask you.'

'Ma, I don't feel like talking.'

'What's the matter? Are you sick? Do you think you've picked up some disease? That's what you're asking for, you know.'

'Ma, I don't have any disease. I killed a man tonight.'

'You did what?'

'I killed a man. It was self-defence. People were there and saw. I just want to go to bed.'

'How could you do such a thing?'

'He didn't give me much of a choice. If I hadn't killed him, you'd be talking to a ghost right now. Now, please, move out of the way. I'm going to bed.'

She stepped aside and he climbed the stairs. The door to the downstairs study opened and Richard Swearingen walked into the hall.

'You heard?' she asked.

'I heard. He said it was self-defence. I believe him.'

'Is this the kind of son you wanted? Are you happy now?'

'No one likes to see people killed. But sometimes it happens. It sounds as if Andrew is able to take care of himself. But if he needs a lawyer, I can get the best in the country.'

'I thought John Tisdale was the best in the country.'

Swearingen said nothing. He returned to his study and closed the door. Ginevra listened. There was nothing but silence. Usually a coyote would howl and the dogs would bark. But tonight there was only silence. She wanted to hear something, anything to disrupt the silence.

'I thought I left all this, all this violence,' she said aloud. Perhaps Swearingen heard, perhaps not. She didn't care. 'All the killing. I thought I left it behind. Is there never an end to it?'

She leaned against the newel post and put her face in her hands.

Harrison sat in the small room at the front of his cottage, the newspaper open in his hands. The room was sparsely furnished – just a wooden rocking chair, a small couch, and a bed.

'You're going to ruin your eyes trying to read in this dim light,' Penelope used to say.

He lowered the paper and stared at the sofa where she used to sit. The sofa arm was frayed.

'I never gave you much, did I, girl? Did you ever complain? Nope, not once. You'd be proud to know a woman runs the newspaper these days. I must say she does a pretty good job. Yeah, you'd be proud.'

He adjusted the wire-rimmed spectacles on the end of his nose. He listened. Spurs crossed the small front porch. Someone knocked.

'Sheriff, it's me, Stuart.'

Harrison rose and struggled across the floor. He was stiff. He had sat in the rocker too long. He opened the door and Stuart stood before him.

'I'm sorry to bother you, Sheriff.'

'What's the matter?'

'That young Swearingen buck, Andrew, shot and killed a man in the Two Rivers.'

'Come on in. Tell me about it.'

Harrison let himself down slowly into the rocker, and Stuart removed his hat and sat on the couch. It was a new hat, black, stiff. It would take some time to break in, but already it felt good. It was important to have a good hat, to look like someone. And a deputy in Cheyenne needed to look like someone.

To the deputy, the room smelled old, stale. Even with the

windows open, no air stirred. The dim light covered them in yellow.

'Tell me what happened,' Harrison said.

'The man who got killed was a farmer. His name was Sven Burleson.'

'I don't think I know him. But then it's hard to keep up with all the new settlers.'

'There were witnesses,' Stuart said. 'Self-defence. Burleson pulled a gun on Swearingen, and Swearingen killed him.'

'Why? Why would that farmer want to kill Swearingen?'

'Apparently it has something to do with Rose. It's no secret Burleson was sweet on her. I guess Andrew was a paying customer.'

'I ought to close that damn saloon. It's nothing but a whorehouse.'

'There was nothing Dooley could do. I'm pretty certain of that. There's one more thing. Those men on the train were in the saloon at the time.'

'Did they have anything to do with it?'

'No, sir.'

'I don't like that gunslinger. Men like him attract trouble. They don't have to be involved. Just their presence is enough to set things in motion.'

'Maybe Swearingen's foreman, Rayburn, set things in motion. I've heard he's been teaching young Swearingen how to shoot.'

'I'd say Swearingen is a good student. I don't like any of this. First, there's the train robbery. There's this man who's awfully good with a pistol, and no one has heard of him. And now this. That bunch of immigrants won't stand for what happened. That means you and me are going to be in the middle of it. Before we know it, we're going to have a war on our hands.'

'They can't go up against a man like Rayburn.'

'No, but McPherson can. We don't know whose side he'll

be on, but I can guess.'

    'So you think he's going to get involved.'

    'Oh, yeah, he's going to get involved.'

CHAPTER 10

Eloise Endicott sat at her desk in the far corner of the office. The other desk belonged to her reporter, Lawrence Byrd. He was out wandering the streets, supposedly looking for a story. She smiled. What kind of story would he uncover at this late hour? She had to hand it to him. He was dedicated.

From the back room where the press churned out pages, a half dozen young men and women, all still in their teens, hustled to show her pages, to ask questions, to make suggestions, to put out a newspaper. They had come from the small farms and somehow had found their way to her office. They knew how to read and write and so she put them to work. She showed them how to set type, how to run the press. Two of the young ladies had begun selling advertising.

'You're like a mother hen,' Byrd had told her.

Maybe she was. But they were so eager to learn, and she was eager to teach them. Besides, having them around gave her and Byrd the time to search out stories, stories about mysterious newcomers like Ezra McPherson.

On the wall opposite her desk stood shelves loaded with newspapers, many yellowed. The lamps burned dimly and she closed her eyes. She saw Ezra McPherson. And when she saw him, she felt she saw the past. The land, like people, had a past. And that past was connected. She was convinced of that. She was convinced that he was part of that past. In Delmonico's, when she talked with McPherson, she talked with a man who had stopped a train robbery and shot and killed most of the desperadoes. She wanted to know who he was. Stokesbury knew there was a story. That explained his reason for accompanying him. But she had an advantage. She had travelled in the West. She had acquaintances, people who might know, who might remember, Ezra McPherson. Someone would know.

Byrd flung open the door and ran to his desk. His face was flushed. He took out a tablet and started to write.

'What are you so worked up about?' she asked.

'There's been a killing inside the Two Rivers.'

Two of the young women, their hair balled tightly behind their heads, stood at a long wooden table and proofed pages. Byrd's announcement got their attention. They scurried to the back room to tell their friends.

'I don't guess they hear stuff like this on the farm,' Byrd said.

'Are you serious – about the killing?' Eloise said.

'Dead serious. Do you like the pun?'

'Not especially.'

'I've got the lead story for the next edition.'

She liked his determination. Cheyenne would not keep him. He was too good. His stories brimmed with life – in this case, death – on the frontier. One day he would hear from a newspaper back East, and she would lose him.

The door opened again, and she saw something she never expected to see. Ezra McPherson walked in. His two travelling companions followed, accompanied by another man she did not recognize.

'Welcome, gentlemen,' she said. 'I was hoping you would

stop by.'

Byrd looked up from his desk.

'These men were there,' Byrd said.

'Where?'

'In the Two Rivers.'

'My reporter tells me there's been a killing.'

'Your reporter tells you correctly,' Marcus said. 'Front-page news, right-hand column.'

'Lawrence, hurry up and start on the linotype. Gentlemen, how can I help you? Mr McPherson, you look like a man who is ready to be interviewed.'

'I don't believe so.'

'If it's not too much trouble, ma'am,' Luke said, 'I'd like to read the article about my brother's murder.'

Luke followed her to the wall of shelves. From one of the middle shelves she pulled a stack of newspapers and laid them on a table and flipped through them. She pulled one paper free and pointed to the article in the narrow right-hand column with a large black headline: 'Man Killed in Alley.' Multiple subheads led into the story.

'I'm not sure it will tell you what you want to know,' she said. 'But you're welcome to read it.'

'Thank you, Mrs. . . .'

'It's Miss Endicott.'

'Yes, well, thank you.'

'Miss Endicott, permit me to introduce myself,' Owen said. 'Owen Chesterfield of Chicago.'

'It's a pleasure, Mr Chesterfield. Do you shoot as well as Mr McPherson?'

'I don't believe so, ma'am.'

'So you're acquainted with his marksmanship. Where have you seen him shoot?'

'You're good, Miss Endicott,' Owen said. 'Perhaps I've only heard about his marksmanship.'

'Perhaps. Mr Stokesbury, I want you to pay special attention to my desk,' she said.

'All right,' he said, and he saw nothing special about it.

'A friend of mine who runs the *Territorial Enterprise* in Virginia City gave it to me as a gift. He respected my journalism integrity, I suppose. This is the desk Samuel Clemens used.'

Marcus walked to the desk and ran his fingers across the scratched surface marred by the black scars left by cigarettes and cigars. He imagined Clemens sitting at the desk, planning his next satiric barb.

'I'm impressed,' he said.

She looked at Ezra. He was not impressed. She could tell. She wondered whether he even knew who Samuel Clemens was. Ezra looked about the office. Something else was obvious. He did not want to look at her.

'Lawrence, who was killed?' she asked.

'This farmer who had taken a liking to one of the girls. His name was Sven Burleson.'

'Let me guess – the killer had taken a liking to the same girl.'

'That was the case.'

'And who is the killer?'

Byrd stopped writing and turned around.

'None other than Andrew Swearingen.'

'Andrew Swearingen?'

'That's right. Rich New York boy kills his first man.'

'Gentlemen, I told you something about the young Mr Swearingen. I must admit I didn't think he would become a killer, at least not yet.'

'It was self-defence,' Byrd said.

'I'm sure that makes Mr Burleson feel better.'

Byrd returned to his tablet. He pushed the pencil as if he would forget the facts at any moment. He had to make sure he included everything.

Marcus walked about the office and stopped at the back door.

'Our linotype is in the back,' she said. 'Go take a look. Lawrence is much better at the keys than I am.'

Marcus walked into the back room, and Ezra stood at the rail that separated her desk from the rest of the office. Luke turned to the jump page where the article continued.

'John was shot in the back,' Luke said.

'I'm not sure that changes anything,' Ezra said.

'The sheriff isn't going to do anything.'

'It's hard to do anything when nobody will talk,' Eloise said.

'But somebody has to know something.'

'Of course, somebody knows something,' she said. 'But that doesn't mean he's going to talk. Talking means repercussions, and most people don't want to deal with repercussions. Are you of the same opinion, Mr McPherson?'

'Yes, ma'am, I'm of the same opinion.'

'Owen, this is your line of work, isn't it?' Luke asked. 'Can't you do something?'

'Well, son, it's not exactly my line of work. There's not really anything I can do. There's not really anything any of us can do. Give the sheriff some credit, son. He's been in the law a long time. Sometimes it takes a while for someone to come forward. When he does, I believe Harrison will act.'

'And what is your profession, Mr Chesterfield?' Eloise asked.

'I'm a Pinkerton, ma'am.'

'A Pinkerton? Why would a Pinkerton man deem it necessary to come to Cheyenne?'

'I'm here just to strike up old acquaintances and do a little reminiscing.'

Outside the front window a slender silhouette stood. The

red tip of a cigarette glowed in the darkness. Eloise stared. In the heat of the August night the newspaper office seemed suddenly cold.

Ezra walked to the door.

'Ezra, maybe you shouldn't open it,' Owen said.

Ezra pulled his coat back and rested his hand on his Colt revolver and opened the door. He stepped onto the sidewalk. No one was there. He looked up and down the street. Only cowboys going in and out of the saloons. He went back inside.

'Mr McPherson, are ghosts following you?' Eloise asked.

'It was just a cowpoke looking for a saloon,' Ezra said.

'I like the possibility of a ghost better,' Owen said. 'There's more of a sense of mystery. It seemed to get cold in here. Did anyone else notice?'

'You're getting old,' Ezra said. 'Old people get cold easily.'

'Well, you aren't a spring chicken.'

Luke read the article again. His eyes moved from one subhead to another, from one paragraph to another, and his fists tightened. Tomorrow he would claim his brother's body. Soon both would be on the eastbound, and the killer would still be roaming Wyoming a free man. No, maybe he wouldn't be on the eastbound. Ezra would protest. But the killer was out there. Luke would find him. He owed it to his brother. He would find him.

Marcus and Luke returned to their hotel rooms, but Ezra and Owen stood in the middle of the street. The saloons were quiet. Cheyenne had gone to bed for the night.

'It was too bad about that farm boy,' Owen said. 'Losing his life like that. Senseless. Completely senseless. We've seen a lot of that kind of killing, haven't we, Ezra?'

'I'm too restless to turn in. Let's walk.'

They walked to the depot. For no particular reason – their

feet just seemed to take them there. No trains stood on the tracks. No passengers congregated on the platform. There was only the silence that was left in the wake of greetings and embraces. They stood in the yard where, earlier, homesteaders had greeted their families, had loaded their belongings, and had started the journey toward a new life in the promised land.

'As soon as you can, get Luke and his brother on the train,' Owen said. 'I'm afraid he's going to do something we'll all regret.'

'I promised his father I'd get him back home in one piece.'

'And old man Tisdale believes it. He thinks a lot of you, Ezra.'

'I owe him a lot.'

'It's damn funny the way things work out,' Owen said.

He lit a cigar and offered one to Ezra.

Ezra smoked and stared at the depot. Never had he expected to see something like this in the West. In the darkness it was a monument to progress. Times had changed. He had been gone what seemed like a lifetime, and during that absence the West had transformed itself into something he almost didn't recognize.

'You said some good things to Luke about the sheriff,' Ezra said. 'But what do you really know about him?'

'Harrison? Oh, he's all right. He was a good enough lawman in his day. He knew how to stay alive. He should take off his badge. He's getting too old for that kind of work.'

'You're older than he is.'

'Yeah, and I'm too old for Pinkerton work.'

'Then why do it?'

'What am I going to do?'

'Run a store.'

Owen laughed.

'Can you see me behind a counter? I'm not as lucky as you.

You get to manage a hunting preserve. That's a little better than a store.'

'The people you deal with in a store are a notch above the people I deal with.'

'How can you say that? The people you deal with are rich.'

'That's my point.'

'Most of them are rich Yankees,' Owen said. 'That's what you mean. You don't like dealing with rich Yankees. You prefer poor Yankees like me.'

They headed back toward the hotel. They were in no hurry.

'We're supposed to have dinner with a man named Swearingen tomorrow,' Ezra said.

'Richard Swearingen.'

'You know him?'

'I've heard about him. You should like him. He's another rich Yankee. It's hard to say who's richer – him or J.P. Morgan. Watch your step around him. He can be brutal. At least that's his reputation. It looks like his son takes after him.'

They walked past the gentlemen's club. All the windows were dark.

'I've heard about that place,' Owen said. 'Rivals anything in New York.'

'Somebody is watching.'

'Where? I don't see anybody.'

'Somebody is at the corner upstairs window.'

'Now how the hell do you know that? I can't see anything. It's dark.'

'If you live long enough in the dark, you learn to see in it.'

'Have you been studying philosophy? I'm impressed. Of course, philosophers don't normally shoot the way you do.'

They stopped at the steps of the hotel.

'Aren't you coming in?' Owen asked. 'Old men like us need our sleep.'

80

'I'll be in later.'

Owen went inside. Ezra sat on the steps and smoked the cigar and looked up and down the street. He listened for the familiar sounds of long ago, but they were gone. They were only a distant memory.

CHAPTER 11

The front room of Slade's Funeral Parlor was small and hot and Owen ran a red handkerchief across his face. Marcus sat in a straight chair and stared at the door that led to the back room where the body of John Tisdale had been kept – preserved – awaiting the arrival of his brother. Marcus wondered just how good Slade was when it came to preservation, especially in the heat of the Wyoming summer.

'I've sometimes wondered why they call a mortuary a parlour,' Owen said. 'A parlour is for a social get-together. Stokesbury, don't you agree?'

'I've never thought about it.'

'But you see my point.'

'Yes, I do. I guess it's just a euphemism.'

'A what?'

'A euphemism.'

'You newspaper people use too many fancy words.'

'Well, we're not supposed to. But what you're talking about is a euphemism.'

'While you folks ride out to the Swearingen place, I'm going to find a store that sells dictionaries. If you're going to throw out big words, I want to be able to look them up.'

'If I contribute to your intellectual pursuits, I'm pleased.'

The door to the back room opened, and Luke appeared,

his face white. He hurried out. Ezra followed. He too looked ill.

'Shouldn't we go after him?' Marcus asked.

'No,' Ezra said. 'Let him be. He needs to be alone for a spell.'

Slade walked into the outer room. He was thin. But the thing Marcus would always remember was his nose. It was long and crooked and hooked at the end.

'When will you be heading East?' Slade asked.

His voice was high-pitched, scratchy. Marcus thought a finger nail on a chalk board sounded more appealing.

'I reckon tomorrow,' Ezra said.

'I'll have everything ready. Good day, gentlemen.'

Slade returned to the back room, and Ezra and Marcus and Owen walked outside. Luke turned the corner and went past other buildings. These, unlike the ones close to the hotel, were mostly one-storey. They stood empty, but Luke didn't notice. He quickened his pace. Dust covered his dark brown shoes. He went past the livery. Old men squatted in the shade near the gate of the corral. They stopped their conversation long enough to spit tobacco and to watch Luke. They thought he was with the man on the train, the man who shot the desperadoes. They couldn't be sure. Their eyesight wasn't what it once was, but they were pretty sure. He was a stranger. Yes, he had come with the gunslinger. They were now sure. Just talking about it made them sure. And their talk shifted to the gunslinger. They wondered just who he was. Somebody from the past. Surely they had seen him before, but no one could remember.

A phaeton hurried past Luke. He didn't notice that either. The sun beat down on him and he struggled to take in a deep breath. He felt faint. He wanted to cry but there were no tears. In the middle of the road he stopped.

'Dr Tisdale.'

He turned and saw the schoolhouse. Jennifer Beauchamp, with a broom in one hand, stood on the front steps. With the other hand, she shielded her eyes from the sun. She came down the steps.

'Dr Tisdale, is everything all right?'

He looked briefly at the road beneath his feet and then he looked away. He didn't want her to see his face.

'Please forgive me. Right now I look like a sorry spectacle.'

'Nonsense. Come into the school. I'll go to the well and get you some water.'

'Please don't go to any trouble. But water would be nice. Just show me where the well is.'

She led him to the well at the side of the schoolhouse, a large, plain, red-brick, square building. He lowered the dark oak bucket. It splashed and he hauled it upward. She handed him a tin cup.

'It's cold,' he said. 'I didn't think anything could be cold in this country. I really appreciate it. How is your son?'

'Bobby is fine. He asked about you and your friend this morning. He wants to know when you're coming to visit us. I'm afraid to say, but he wants your friend to teach him how to shoot. He's too young.'

'Your son is a fine boy.'

'I think my husband would be proud of him.'

The cup was cold in his hand, and he drank again.

'Dr Tisdale, what is wrong? I don't guess it's any of my business, but if I can help, I'd like to.'

'I was just at Slade's Funeral Parlor. I needed to make arrangements for my brother. Being there with him – I didn't expect it to affect me the way it did. I just started thinking about the good times we had together, times we would never repeat. He was a wonderful brother. I had to get out. I've been around death a lot. As a doctor it's kind of hard to avoid it. So I can't explain what happened.'

'You don't need to explain. I understand. He was your brother.'

'He was murdered. Everyone around here seems so damn – excuse my language – so damn helpless when it comes to solving a crime.'

'Please don't get involved in whatever led to your brother's death. I didn't know your brother, of course, but I'm sure he wouldn't want you to do something that could get you. . . .'

'Killed? No, I'm not worried about that. Besides, I have Ezra to look after me.'

They realized they were not alone. Ezra stood behind them. He removed his hat.

'Good morning, ma'am. Luke, Curly saw you stop here. He passed you in a phaeton. He's ready to take us to Swearingen's. Are you up to it?'

'I'm fine, Ezra. Mrs Beauchamp, I was thirsty, and you gave me water. I thank you for that. I have to go. We're supposed to have dinner with the man my brother worked for.'

'Then you should be going.'

Luke and Ezra joined Eloise in the back of the phaeton. Marcus sat next to Curly. With a snap of the reins, Curly sent the two chestnut mares plunging into the heat of the morning. Jennifer came to the front steps and watched. The phaeton disappeared in a cloud of dust.

Soon the town was behind them. Before them stretched the prairie, vast, endless, implacable, reaching toward the far mountains. Herds of cattle grazed on the parched grass. Some sought shelter beneath cottonwoods and white oaks. Marcus expected to see ranch hands, but there were none.

Whiskey bottle after whiskey bottle Andrew set on the fence post and stepped back. He drew and fired and the glass shattered. The morning sun threw heat, merciless and unforgiving, on the land, but Andrew did not mind. He did not think about it. All he could see was Sven Burleson writhing on the dirty floor of the Two Rivers, blood spilling from his gut. He still heard the groans, and he hoped the sound of bottles breaking into shards would drive memories of last night into oblivion. With his shirt sleeve he wiped his eyes. He was crying and he did not understand. He shot more bottles and still he wept.

Ginevra stood at the bannister of the second-floor gallery outside her bedroom door and watched her son. White puffs flew from the barrel of his .45. With each shot she trembled. Finally she walked back into her bedroom.

Swearingen pushed open the gate and lumbered across the brown stiff grass. His shadow slid across the land, and Andrew holstered the pistol.

'Looks like Rayburn taught you well,' Swearingen said. 'Those bottles don't stand a chance.'

'The farm boy in the saloon last night didn't stand a chance either. I reckon you know all about it.'

'I heard you talking to your mother. You said it was self-defence.'

'He's dead. I woke up this morning knowing I had killed a man.'

'It's a hard land, Andrew. Men sometimes have to kill. When I was in the war, I had to kill. If I had chosen not to, I wouldn't be standing here today. Sometimes, if you want to survive in this world, you have to kill. Andrew, look at me. Are you crying?'

'I didn't think I'd feel like this.'

'Believe me – I know how you feel. I remember when I killed my first man in the war. It was the first day at Gettysburg. I'll never forget the look in his eyes. It was as if he was saying to me, "I can't believe I'm killed by a Yankee." Well, a Yankee killed him. And he was not the only Reb this Yankee killed.'

86

'But, Father, I thought if I proved myself with a gun, I'd feel like a man. That's not how I feel, not at all. I feel empty, hollow.'

'You'll get over it,' Swearingen said. 'Stop crying. Rayburn is taking some men out this morning. I want you to go with them. It'll get your mind off last night.'

'What will we be doing?'

'Just looking after some of our cattle. A little rustling has been going on. We need to look into the matter. Nothing too serious, but it'll help to clear your head.'

Swearingen slapped his son on the shoulder.

'How about it?'

'Sure. Whatever you say.'

'No more crying.'

'No more crying.'

The heat was relentless. Curly kept a tight grip on the reins and urged the two mares into a faster gallop. Eloise held on to her blue hat.

'What's the hurry, Curly?' Eloise asked.

'The sooner we get there, the sooner we're out of the heat, ma'am.'

They put miles behind them. How many – Marcus had no idea. It seemed they had been in the phaeton all day. They came to a wide, shallow river.

'I'm going to let these ladies cool off and have a drink,' Curly said.

The phaeton sat in the middle of the river. Just beyond them it forked.

'What river is this?' Marcus asked.

'The Medicine Bow River,' Curly said. 'You see that fork? Legend has it the Lakota Sioux had a big powwow here years ago. Some wanted to go due north to the Black Hills. Even though they knew they'd have fighting to do, that's where they wanted to go. But then some of the elders wanted to go to the northwest, to try to get away from war. They went due north.'

'We don't have to worry about the Sioux now, do we?' Marcus asked.

'We've got problems, but the Sioux ain't one of them.'

Ezra stepped down into the water. A small herd of cows drank not far away, and they lifted their heads and stared. His leather boots moved through the water and up the small embankment.

'Ezra, what are you doing?' Luke called out.

Curly urged the mares forward. Once the phaeton crossed to the other side, Eloise jumped down and followed Ezra. He stood in the sun-hardened field and stared at the fork.

'It's awfully hot, Mr McPherson, to stop and admire the scenery,' Eloise said.

'Ezra. You can call me that.'

'All right. Ezra, it's hot out here in the middle of nowhere.'

'I just wanted – I just wanted to stand on this land, to feel it beneath my feet. I don't reckon that makes any sense.'

'Yes, it makes sense. The more I get to know you, the more sense it makes. It's been a long time since you've been in the West, hasn't it?'

He turned and looked at her.

'You don't have to answer,' she said. 'I already know the answer.'

A breeze stirred. It came from the north. It followed the north fork south. It came quickly and then it was gone.

'It's a beautiful land,' he said.

'The grass is brittle.'

'It's still beautiful.'

'Maybe you should stay. Luke can take his brother back East. Maybe you were meant to stay here. You're a man of the West. And no matter where you go, you'll always be that. You can't escape it.'

He stared once more at the expanse of prairie.

'We should go,' he said.

The others were relieved when Ezra and Eloise climbed back into the phaeton. Marcus realized he had just learned something. There was something about Ezra that Eloise understood. She knew exactly the reason Ezra wanted to walk the land.

'Ezra, you all right?' Luke asked.

Ezra nodded, and the phaeton raced on.

CHAPTER 12

The thing Marcus would remember years later about the Swearingen house was its size. He didn't think he had ever seen a house so big. Double galleries encircled it. Richard Swearingen waited at the top of the steps. He was large too. He didn't just walk down the steps to the phaeton. It seemed he moved as one big mass, sort of the way glaciers moved. At least that's what Marcus had read about glaciers. Swearingen extended his large hand to Eloise. She smiled a smile that said, 'I know you don't want me here, but here I am anyway.'

'Miss Endicott, I'm glad you could join us,' Swearingen said.

'But did you have to send a phaeton? They're dangerous.'

'Nonsense. Not when they're in the right hands. And Curly is an expert. Isn't that right, Curly?'

'Yes, sir. I can handle a phaeton.'

'See – there's no danger,' Swearingen said. 'You must be Luke Tisdale. I'd recognize you anywhere. You have your brother's eyes. And I bet you're Marcus Stokesbury, reporter for the *Atlanta Constitution*. You're a long way from home, Mr Stokesbury. And you must be Ezra McPherson, defender of the Union Pacific. I've been hearing about you. Please come in and get out of this unmerciful sun.'

'I'd say he's done his homework,' Marcus said.

'A man with his money does his homework,' Luke said.

Swearingen led them down the dark entry hall and into the parlour.

The phaeton lurched toward the barn. Simmons shouted a greeting and took the reins, and Curly jumped down. Simmons had hurt his back, so he wasn't riding. He was too old to be working on the ranch, but Curly liked him. He thought his scruffy beard made for a friendly face. But the important thing was Curly thought he could trust him, and he couldn't say that about too many folks.

'Where's Rayburn?' Curly asked.

'Him and a bunch of others headed out awhile ago, including that young Swearingen fellow. I asked Rayburn which range he was going to, but you know Rayburn. Half the time he doesn't care to answer an honest question. This morning was one of those times. One thing's for certain – he had a determined look on his face. Did you have any trouble heading back?'

'No. I wasn't expecting any trouble. Have you heard something?'

'There's talk, Curly, a lot of talk about a range war. Men like Swearingen are used to pushing folks around. I don't think those homesteaders aim to be pushed around.'

In the parlour, Swearingen and his guests sat in chairs with ornate carvings. Long, heavy navy, almost black, drapes covered the tall windows. No sunlight crept in. A young woman soon entered. Black braids fell beneath her shoulders. She was small, slender. She did not smile. She did not look at their faces.

'Will you folks have something to drink?' Swearingen asked. 'Lee-Sun can provide some awfully tasty concoctions.'

'Just water,' Eloise said, and the others agreed that water would be fine.

'Yes, I'm sure you're all parched dry after the ride out

91

here. Lee-Sun, please bring these folks some water.'

Soon she returned with a silver tray bearing crystal glasses filled with water.

'Thank you for inviting us,' Luke said.

'No need to thank me. I was happy to do it. Luke, I knew your brother well. He was like a son. A brilliant legal mind. In New York I relied on his advice. I did out here too. I can't tell you how shocked and saddened I was by his death. Somebody will get to the bottom of it, I assure you.'

'Do you think Sheriff Harrison is that somebody?' Luke asked.

'I guess that remains to be seen.'

Marcus looked about the parlour. It was not quite what he expected in a Wyoming ranch house. It looked more like his vision of a New York drawing room – plush velvet cushions, Persian rug in the centre. He expected to see photographs sitting on the mantle. There were none, only a cherry clock that ticked loudly.

'I once met Henry Grady,' Swearingen said. 'He was speaking in New York. A dynamic speaker he was. Because of him, I invested in textile mills in Atlanta and Augusta.'

'The state of Georgia appreciates the investment,' Marcus said.

'Well, the thing that will truly bring this country back together is commerce. Put money in people's pockets and they will forget about the war. Do you agree, Mr McPherson?'

'Money can't make some people forget some things,' Ezra said.

'No, but it can help. It's been twenty-three years now. The country still needs healing, and prosperity can get the job done. Mr McPherson, did you fight in the war?'

'Yes, I fought.'

'And, considering the way you can shoot, you probably sent many a man to meet his maker.'

Swearingen was the only one who laughed. Marcus looked at Ezra. His face was hard.

'Ah, here at last are some members of my family,' Swearingen said.

Ezra, Marcus, and Luke stood. Through the door walked Peter and Anne Swearingen and Ginevra Swearingen.

'Let me introduce my son, Peter, and his lovely wife, Anne. I have one other son, Andrew, but he won't be joining us today. And this is my wife, Ginevra. I believe we all know the esteemed editor of our newspaper, Eloise Endicott. Here we have Ezra McPherson, Marcus Stokesbury and Luke Tisdale, John's brother.'

Just inside the door, Ginevra stopped.

'Ginevra dear, are you all right?' Swearingen asked. 'You look as if you've seen a ghost.'

Ginevra sat on the settee.

'Yes, I'm fine. It's the heat. No matter how much time I spend out here, I'll never grow accustomed to it.'

'I had heard you were from Missouri,' Eloise said.

'Yes, but I still hate the heat.'

'It's all those dark dresses you're so fond of wearing,' Swearingen said. 'You should wear something lighter. You look as if you're in mourning.'

'I understand you're a doctor,' Peter said. 'As you can see, my wife is going to need a doctor soon.'

'Doc Grierson will do a good job,' Anne said.

'If he's sober.'

'Peter, really.'

'Luke, have you had any experience delivering babies?'

'Some.'

'We may call upon you.'

'We're not going to be in Cheyenne long,' Ezra said.

'I see,' Peter said. 'As long as you're here, though, keep your bag ready – just in case.'

'We'll be fine,' Anne said.

'My son worries too much,' Swearingen said. 'He takes after his mother. I believe it's time we eat.'

They went down the hall into the dining room and sat at a long mahogany table and ate steak, the primary Wyoming course, Marcus decided. At one end of the table Swearingen sat, at the other end Ginevra. She did not look up. Ezra just picked at his meal. Luke was puzzled. He had never seen Ezra struggle with a meal.

'Luke, I've known your father a long time,' Swearingen said. 'I provided the financing for the expansion of his steel works. It was a good investment. But then I knew it would be.'

'Father has to talk business,' Peter said.

'What's wrong with that? This country runs on business. Luke, your father has tried to get me to visit him on Jekyll. Is it as beautiful as he says it is?'

'It's a paradise,' Luke said. 'Ezra manages the hunting preserve. If you come, he'll show you how to shoot quail.'

'Mr McPherson, you're good at shooting more than quail. Where did you learn to shoot the way you do?'

'I just picked it up along the way,' Ezra said.

'Along the way? And where might be the way? Where do you hail from?'

'A lot of places.'

Ginevra looked up. Her face was pale. And Eloise saw.

'When it comes to guns, my wife doesn't like to hear about them,' Swearingen said. 'I keep telling her it's a hard world. Do you agree, Mr McPherson? Do you believe it's a hard world?'

'Yes. It's a hard world.'

'And because it's a hard world, bad things happen to good people – bad things happen to good people like your brother, Luke. There's just no accounting for it. But one thing I keep emphasizing to my boys – because it's such a hard world,

94

we've got to be hard ourselves, assuming we want to survive. Not everyone is going to survive. Just take those immigrants, those homesteaders – and believe me, I wish you would take them away from here – they have no idea what they're in for. As hot as it is now, it's freezing in the winter. Not all of them are going to survive. Oh, right now, they think they will. But I'm telling you – they won't.'

Luke did not answer. He had met the man his brother worked for. They had talked. He had nothing more to say. Somehow he found it difficult to believe that his brother had worked for this man. He wanted to leave.

'I've learned that in finance only the fit survive,' Swearingen said. 'That's why you have your Rockefellers and your Carnegies and your Tisdales. Luke, your father knows exactly what I'm talking about. Was he going to let some anarchists tell him how to run his railroad? No. He dealt with it the way he should have dealt with it. After a few of the troublemakers got walloped on the head, they settled down. Yes, sir, whether you're talking about Wall Street or the Wyoming frontier, only the fit are going to survive. It's that simple. Mr McPherson, you look like a man who understands. Don't you think what I'm saying makes sense?'

'Perhaps Mr McPherson is tired of answering questions,' Ginevra said. 'Perhaps we're all tired of speeches.'

'Mr Swearingen, what made you decide to leave New York and go into ranching?' Marcus asked.

'I haven't left New York for good. Wyoming is just another opportunity. I'm not the only Easterner out here. We've put a lot of money into the economy. We're raising the best beef cattle you'll find anywhere. I know Texans will argue with me, but I stand by what I said. And we've got the railroad. It's easy to ship the cattle to market. The biggest problem is the weather. We can't seem to catch a break. I guess you noticed the pasture coming out here. Dry and brittle.'

After the dinner Swearingen sent Sun-Lee to find Curly. Ezra excused himself from the table and stepped onto the lower front veranda to light a cigarette. He looked toward the barn. In the corral a mare and filly trotted. An old man leaned against the fence and watched.

Suddenly he knew he was not alone, and he turned quickly, his hand on his Colt.

'You're not going to shoot me, are you? I'm not a train robber.'

Ginevra stood beside him.

'I just wasn't expecting someone to follow me out here.'

'I need to talk to you.'

'Then talk.'

'Not here. Somewhere else.'

Ezra inhaled the cigarette smoke and released it slowly.

'What will your husband say?'

'He doesn't care what I do. Besides, he told me he's going to the gentlemen's club tonight. He'll be in Cheyenne till morning. He'll find something there to keep him occupied.'

'I don't see any good that can come from talking.'

'Please. You crossed the Medicine Bow River coming out here. There's a fork. It's called the Lakota Sioux Fork.'

'Yes, I know. Curly told us the story.'

'Above the fork is a hill. There's a cottonwood tree. I ride there sometimes when I want to get away. I'll meet you at nine.'

Curly drove the phaeton out of the barn and pulled up to the front steps.

'Sun-Lee says you folks are ready to head back to town.'

'I'll get the others,' Ginevra said.

Ezra flipped the cigarette onto the dirt.

'You know, Mr McPherson, we've got a foreman that may know you,' Curly said.

'Is that a fact? What's his name?'

96

'Rayburn. He's from Missouri. Ever heard of him?'

Ezra stared at Curly. The cowboy wished he had kept his mouth shut. But he was curious. He had to know. The look on Ezra's face gave him the answer he was looking for.

'Is he around?'

'No. This is a big spread. He stays busy.'

'I bet he does.'

Voices came down the dark hall. Swearingen laughed. The door swung open and he slapped Luke on the back.

'We've got plenty of room in Cheyenne for docs,' he said. 'Old Doc Grierson won't mind. Besides, folks don't call him old for nothing. He doesn't move too fast. Consider hanging up a shingle here.'

'I'll consider it.'

'Curly, watch how you drive this thing,' Eloise said. 'I want to get back to Cheyenne in one piece.'

Swearingen stood on the veranda and waved. Ezra looked over his shoulder. Ginevra was nowhere to be seen.

CHAPTER 13

Cliff Darton could think of a lot of things he'd rather do than hunt for a heifer and return it to the herd. For one thing, he would love to jump off his mare and plunge into the cold waters of the wide clear branch that ran through the pasture. But the heifer had gone missing, and his pa told him what he had to do, so he did it. When his pa said something, that was the end of it. No discussion. The early afternoon sun kept him in its sights. There was no escape.

The heifer seemed happy to be back in the fold, and Cliff couldn't help grinning. It was a good herd – not large, but it was growing. Maybe Maggie would realize he was a young man with prospects. Her pa's ranch joined his pa's, so it would be easy enough for her to see that the Dartons were going to prosper. It didn't matter that he was only sixteen. Of course, it seemed to matter to Maggie's pa. But Cliff knew cattle. The Dartons had raised plenty of cattle back in Arkansas. Opportunities were better in Wyoming. He was going to make something of himself. Maggie's pa would see.

'Jody, how much longer you gonna be?' Cliff asked.

His younger brother, only twelve, had gone into nearby

bushes at the edge of a dry creek bed.

'Gimme a minute. I'm glad we brought some pages out of that catalogue.'

At first Cliff didn't see the riders on the crest of the hill. They were almost upon him before he realized it.

'We got company,' Cliff said. 'Stay in the bushes. Don't come out. You hear me?'

'Who are they, Cliff?'

'I don't know. Stay in the bushes.'

Rayburn, Andrew, and two other riders reined their horses and studied the herd.

'What do you men want?' Cliff asked.

'What's your name, boy?' Rayburn asked.

'Cliff Darton.'

'Here's one with the Swearingen brand,' one of Rayburn's men said.

'You certain?' Rayburn asked.

The rider tossed his lariat around the cow's neck and led her to Rayburn, who ran his hand over the black S.

'Boy, what are you doing with one of Mr Swearingen's cows?' Rayburn said.

'Mister, I don't know how she got here,' Cliff said. 'Swearingen's cows roam all over the prairie.'

'Maybe you decided to do a little cattle rustling. Maybe you thought we wouldn't miss just one cow. But it don't matter if you rustle one cow or a whole herd – rustling is still rustling.'

'I ain't never rustled no cattle.'

'You alone, boy?'

'Yeah, I'm alone.'

'Then who does that pinto belong to?' Rayburn asked.

One of the ranch hands rode slowly into the brush and flushed the young boy. He ran up to his brother.

'I thought you said you were alone,' Rayburn said. 'You're not only a rustler. You're also a liar.'

Cliff was afraid. He didn't want anything to happen to his brother. Then the blow from the butt of a rifle struck him in the side of the head. His hat flew off and he tumbled out of his saddle and his brother screamed. Another one of the men grabbed him and lifted him to his feet and tied his hands behind him. Blood streamed down his face. Jody cried, ran to the man who had hit his brother and pounded his fists against the leather chaps. A boot to the chest sent him sprawling.

'Don't do this,' Cliff said.

'This looks like a good, sturdy limb,' one of the riders said.

'I don't think this is a good idea,' Andrew said. 'We don't know that he took the cow.'

'To hell we don't.'

The rider tossed a rope across a limb. Another rider slipped the noose around Cliff's head and he tightened it.

'Special knot for cattle rustlers,' the rider said.

The two men who rode with Andrew and Rayburn heaved Cliff back onto the saddle.

'Please, Mister, you're making a mistake.'

'The man who steals cattle makes the mistake,' Rayburn said.

'He doesn't look like a rustler,' Andrew said. 'Let him do some explaining.'

'Andrew, you really think you know what a rustler looks like? Did you have a lot of experience with rustlers in New York? Your daddy wants me to get rid of these varmints. If you ain't got the stomach for it, then go back to your mama.'

A rider slapped the horse with his hat and it galloped away, past the pinto, past the bushes.

'Cliff!' Jody cried.

Cliff swung wildly at first. His feet kicked. Then they grew still.

'Well, that's one rustler we won't have to worry about any

more,' Rayburn said.

Tears streaked down Jody's face, but he said nothing. He stared at his brother, his head cocked to one side, the eyes open in fear and disbelief.

'Boy, you're lucky we ain't stringing you up,' Rayburn said. 'Tell your folks this is what's going to happen to all you rustlers.'

Rayburn and the two ranch hands rode toward the hills. Andrew hesitated. He looked down at the boy. He thought about the night before, the man he killed, and he felt the nausea again. Hate burned in his eyes.

'I. . . . I'm sorry,' Andrew said. 'I didn't mean for this to happen. Do you believe me, boy? Say something. Please – please say something.'

Jody did not speak. Andrew spurred his horse and followed the others.

Jody ran his shirt sleeve across his eyes. He looked into the distance. The riders blended into the base of the hills. All that he could see was the distant dust kicked up by the horses' hoofs. Andrew – he would remember the name.

Curly wanted to go faster, but Eloise made herself clear. She did not want to go fast. She had no desire to be toppled onto the Wyoming prairie. This is just annoying, he said to himself. She just doesn't appreciate a good pair of horses which are comfortable hitched to a phaeton. He wanted to explain it to her, but it wouldn't do any good.

Luke was quiet. In fact, he hadn't said a word since they left the Swearingen place. Marcus figured he was still thinking about his brother, and why shouldn't he? But Luke was not the only quiet one. Ezra was silent too, and Marcus wondered whether his silence had anything to do with Ginevra Swearingen. He noticed the way they looked at each other. They had known each other before. Marcus was sure of it.

They probably had never expected to see each other again. She was from Missouri. Now Marcus knew something else about Ezra.

At the top of a distant hill, a rider sat on a pinto and waved his floppy hat, not gently, and Eloise saw.

'There's someone on the hill,' she said. 'You see him? He's waving at us.'

'It looks like a boy,' Luke said.

'I don't think he's waving hello,' Ezra said.

'Curly, head up that hill,' Eloise said.

'I don't think we oughtta get involved in anything,' Curly said.

'Do as the lady says,' Ezra said.

The phaeton left the road and cut across the grassland to the base of the hill. The boy still waved his hat. Curly cracked the whip and the horses pulled harder. Marcus took one look at the boy's face and realized he was frantic.

'Boy, what's the matter?' Eloise asked.

'It's my brother.'

Jody led them down the other side of the hill and across the valley. They saw the tree.

'Oh, my God,' Eloise said.

Jody jumped from his horse and ran to his brother and looked up at him.

'Curly, pull up next to him,' Ezra said. 'Stokesbury, you hold his legs while I cut the rope.'

Marcus walked up to the stiff legs, but hesitated. Ezra pulled a knife from his belt and leaned from the seat of the phaeton.

'Stokesbury, grab his legs,' Ezra said.

'I'll help,' Luke said.

They lowered Cliff to the ground and Jody stood beside his brother and wiped the tears. Eloise wrapped her arms about his shoulders.

Marcus stepped back and looked toward the hills. He felt weak.

'What's your name, boy?' Ezra asked.

'Jody,' he said, and he wiped his face on his shirt sleeve. 'That's my brother – Cliff. We're Dartons. We live by Cavendish Creek. Mister, those men said we were cattle rustlers. We never stole no cattle. Cliff tried to tell them, but they wouldn't listen. We never stole no cattle. Mister, you believe me, don't you?'

'Yes, son,' Ezra said. 'I believe you. Curly, where is Cavendish Creek?'

'Not far.'

'Do you know who did this to your brother?' Eloise said.

'They were Swearingen's men. They said one of the cows belonged to Swearingen. One of the men was called Andrew.'

'He gets around,' Ezra said.

Curly turned his head and said nothing.

'Jody, I want you to ride in the phaeton next to Miss Endicott,' Ezra said.

'Yes, sir.'

'Luke, you and Stokesbury help me get this young man on the pinto. I'll tie him across the saddle.'

During the ride to Cavendish Creek, Eloise kept her arm around the boy. Lynching – the word sent a cold shiver throughout her body. There was no reason to murder that boy, she kept saying to herself. She drew Jody closer to her, as if to drive the memory of what had happened out of his head, but she knew he would never forget this day. He would always remember his brother hanging from a tree in the sunlight that scorched the earth.

The Darton homestead didn't amount to much. In the midst of the endless prairie, with the mountains a distant backdrop, the wooden house looked small. A low-slung porch ran across the front. One end sagged lower than the other. A hen and her chickens scurried in front of the phaeton. Not far from the house a small corral sat empty. The door opened and a stooped figure limped across the porch. A woman holding a dish towel followed. She saw the pinto and the burden it bore and screamed. She headed down the three steps, but the man stopped her. He had already seen, and he knew.

Jody jumped from the phaeton and ran to his mother. The father walked up to the pinto and lay a calloused hand on Cliff's back.

'Oh, God. Oh, God,' the woman cried, and Eloise went to her.

'Who did this?' the man asked.

The man was thin. He appeared pale and sickly and Marcus wondered how such a man could survive on the Wyoming plain – especially now, with one son dead and the other not old enough to do what a man needed to do on a struggling ranch. Marcus remembered Swearingen's words about survival.

'It was Swearingens,' Jody said. 'They said we rustled. We never did, Pa.'

'I know you didn't,' the father said.

'We came along and saw Jody,' Eloise said. 'He led us to – to your other son.'

Ezra loosened the ropes and he and Marcus slid the body from the saddle.

'Bring him inside,' Darton said. 'We'll put him on the dining table.'

The one-room house was dark and hot. Marcus looked about. There were only a few chairs. No rug. At one end of the room was a pine dry sink. Marcus surmised the family had brought it with them to this land of hope and opportunity. At the other end of the room threadbare curtains partitioned off what Marcus figured to be bedrooms.

The mother stood next to Cliff and ran her fingers through his hair. Deep furrows ran across her forehead. Her mouth was small, and her thin lips trembled. Her fingers touched the black-purplish rope burn on his neck. The father leaned over the table and shook his head.

'Cliff never did no harm to nobody,' he said.

'I told you not to send him out today,' the mother said.

The man stepped back from the table.

'Why would you not want your son to ride out today, ma'am?' Ezra asked.

'Some of Swearingen's men were here two nights ago,' she said. 'There was this one man they called Rayburn. He seemed to be in charge. We stood out there on the porch and listened to what he had to say. It was dark. It was black. We could see only the outlines of their faces, and they were hideous faces. That much I could tell. There was death about them. I could sense it. They said there was no room for people like us out here. They said we should go back to where we came from – if we knew what was good for us. We told them this was our land. We had paid for it fair and square. We said nobody was going to run us off. He just laughed. He sat on his big black horse and laughed. And then the others laughed. Suddenly he stopped laughing. And his voice was hideous like his face. He told us if we stayed, we might get hurt – or worse. I told Seth not to send the boys out. I didn't want them to get – to get hurt.'

The father dropped into a straight chair and stared at the floor caked with dust. He laid his large, bony hands on his knees. His face was long, gaunt, and it almost rested on his chest.

'Where are you folks from?' Marcus asked.

'Arkansas,' he said. 'Not far from Fort Smith. We heard stories about the opportunity here in Wyoming, so we decided to give it a try. It hasn't turned out the way we expected.'

'Mrs Darton, what can we do to help?' Eloise asked.

'You've done enough. I appreciate it. I'll get my boy cleaned up. We'll give him a proper Christian burial.'

Curly stood just inside the door and stared at the lifeless body on the table. The thing he would remember was the boots, the dirt-caked boots that hung off the end of the table. They were not anything special, but, for some reason, those were the things he would remember.

'I never got your names,' the father said.

'My name is Luke Tisdale,' Luke said. 'This is Eloise Endicott, and Marcus Stokesbury, and Ezra McPherson.'

The father raised his head, and the mother stood straight.

'McPherson,' Darton said.

'You're the man who shot the train robbers,' the mother said.

'One of the neighbours was in town, heard about it,' Darton said. 'He stopped by on the way home and told us all about it.'

'You're what Cheyenne needs,' the mother said. 'For all its wealth, for all its railroad glory, this town is a lawless wasteland. What it needs is a man like you to. . . .'

'Your town has a sheriff,' Ezra said. 'I'm sure he'll make someone pay for what happened to your son.'

'Harrison is too old,' Darton said. 'At least that's what I've been told. I don't personally know the man. But from what I hear, he's not inclined to do anything.'

The mother left her son and walked up to Ezra and looked into his face. She reached up and grasped his shoulders.

'You're an avenger. I can see it in your eyes. You've ridden out of the darkness and you've brought light with you. And you've brought a sword. To end violence, you wield violence. And evil will be cut down. It will perish beneath your blood-stained sword.'

'Ezra, I think we'd best be going,' Luke said.

Ezra laid a hand on Jody's shoulder and then turned and walked away. Curly was already holding the reins. The phaeton pulled away and headed back to Cheyenne.

CHAPTER 14

Meta Anderson stood on the front porch of the two-room, unpainted cabin and stared at what was supposed to be the front yard. Nothing would grow. Her ma and pa had tried, but no grass, no flowers would grow.

'I know. It looks pretty pitiful,' her mother said.

Isabelle Anderson stood in the doorway and wiped her hands on her blue apron and knew what her daughter was thinking.

'It ain't your fault,' Meta said. 'It ain't Pa's fault. The problem's not enough rain. This land is going to dry up and blow away. I just hope I ain't on it when it happens.'

The mother left the doorway and stood beside her daughter.

'I wish you wouldn't say things like that,' she said. 'At least don't say them when your pa's around.'

'He ain't around.'

'He was last night. You said the same thing. It hurt him.'

'I'm sorry, but he should have never brought us out here.'

Isabelle looked off into the distance. Out there, somewhere, in the heat, her husband and three sons were putting up a fence.

'He was following a dream,' Isabelle said. 'Is there anything wrong with that? He wanted something better for us, and he thought this land, with hard work, would provide it.'

'You sound like John.'

Meta hadn't said his name in days, at least not out loud. But now she said it, and she wanted to say it again, as if repeating it would somehow cause him to reappear, to walk up to the porch, to take her hands, and to lead her away.

'I wish I had known him better,' the mother said. 'But when he came here to see you, when he talked, I knew he loved this land, as much as your pa. Your brothers liked him too. It hurt us all when he was killed. You don't expect something bad to happen to someone like him, but it does. There's no explaining it. Meta, I know you're hurting. I'm your ma. You can talk if you want to.'

'His brother has come to take him back East. Sue Beth told me. She heard it at the dinner table. His brother is a doctor. He was on the train that was held up.'

'It must be hard on the brother.'

'This is not what John would have wanted,' Meta said. 'I've never looked at this land the way he did. I know he loved it. He saw possibilities here. I see only something that's desolate. He saw a land where dreams could come true. He would want to be buried here, not back East. His brother should know that.'

'What are you suggesting?' the mother asked.

'I'm suggesting someone should tell the brother.'

'Meta, you are not the someone who should tell him.'

'Ma, his brother should know. I don't want to contradict you, but, yes, I should be the one to tell him.'

'You should do no such thing.'

'I can ride Buttercup into town. It shouldn't be too difficult to find Dr Tisdale.'

'That old mule probably wouldn't make it to town and back, certainly not in this heat.'

Isabelle grasped her daughter's shoulders, held them

tightly, and turned her. She looked into her face, a young face, still beautiful, but already lined by the sun. The pale white cotton fabric on the shoulders was thin and, for a moment, she felt ashamed her daughter had to wear such a dress.

'Ma, John should stay here. Somebody needs to tell the brother, and I'm the only one who will.'

'Listen to me,' Isabelle said. 'This is a dangerous time. The big ranchers don't want us here. What your pa and brothers are doing right now – putting up a fence – is dangerous. They're on our land, yet they don't know but what somebody will ride up and try to shoot them. Your pa has said it's no longer a question of if there's going to be trouble; only when. Don't make matters worse.'

'I don't see how talking to John's brother will make matters worse.'

Meta looked at her mother. The grey eyes were faded, burned by the sun. They were tired. For a moment she hated her father. He brought them here. But that was harsh, as harsh as the sun. She shouldn't hate him. She knew that.

'You loved him, didn't you?' Isabelle asked.

'I'm going to town. I'll be back by supper.'

'What will I tell your pa?'

'Nothing. Tell him nothing.'

The white bonnet did little to protect her face from the sun. She bit into a biscuit her mother forced her to take.

'Buttercup, you sure ain't in much of a hurry,' she said.

She drank from a canteen one of her brothers had left in the house. The water was warm. The land stretched before her, vast, treeless. Mountains stood tall, blue, wraith-like, in the distance, and she remembered John.

'This land is beautiful,' he said. 'I admire your family. I admire all you settlers. You're the ones who are going to make this land something special, something great.'

'If it doesn't kill us first.'

'It won't. You're strong, stronger than you realize.'

She remembered his light brown hair, just beginning to thin on top. She remembered his grey eyes, his soft touch.

'Do you remember the first time you touched me?' she asked.

'I bet you do.'

'Of course, I do. You didn't answer the question, so you don't remember. But that's okay. I'll remember for both of us. I was walking out of Taylor's General Store. My arms were full. You weren't paying attention, and you ran into me. Do you remember now?'

'I seem to recall you ran into me.'

'I dropped a sack of flour. Lucky it didn't spill all over the sidewalk.'

'I picked it up and put it in the back of the wagon. I tipped my hat. See? I remember. Your pa was with you and he didn't look too happy. If he could see us now, sitting here having a picnic, I suspect he wouldn't be too happy.'

'He doesn't know you, John. All he knows is you work for Swearingen. Why do you work for him? I'm sorry. I shouldn't have asked. It's none of my business.'

They lay, supported on their elbows, beside the checkered cloth. Near them the Pawnee Branch wound its way to the Medicine Bow. The water murmured, and Meta remembered it sounded good. Her mother had helped her prepare the lunch. No one had told her pa.

'I'm leaving Swearingen. I haven't told anyone. You're the first.'

'Are you sure this is what you want to do?'

'I'm sure. I can't really discuss it. He's a client, you know. But I want to buy some land and build something. I don't want to go back East. I want this to be my home. This is where

I want to raise a family.'

'You're a lawyer. What do you know about working the land?'

'I'll get a wife who knows how to work the land.'

'You need a mule, not a wife.'

She stopped at the livery and slid down from the mule. She smelled the hay and knew Buttercup would be happy. Old Smitty came out of the stable, his red face streaked with sweat. He wore overalls and walked with a limp.

'Howdy, Smitty.'

'Well, howdy, Miss Meta. Are your folks behind you?'

'No. It's just me.'

'Miss Meta, that's an awfully long way to travel by yourself.'

'I did just fine. Can you take care of Buttercup for a little while?'

'I'd be happy to. Me and Buttercup git along just fine.'

'Smitty, do you know that John Tisdale's brother is in town?'

'Yes, ma'am. I imagine everybody knows him and a gun-slinger are in town. It's created quite a bit of excitement.'

'Do you know where I can find him?'

'You won't have to look far, Miss Meta. There he goes.'

Meta turned. A phaeton raced past the livery.

'Who's driving that thing?'she asked.

'Curly Pike. One of Mr Swearingen's hands. My guess is he's going to stop at the newspaper office. One of his passengers is the newspaper lady. John Tisdale's brother is with them.'

'Thank you, Smitty.'

She left the shade of the stable and headed up the street. She turned a corner and saw the phaeton.

Luke Tisdale offered his hand and helped Eloise onto the sidewalk. She saw the girl. Something about her suggested that she was heading for them. Eloise didn't know what it was,

112

but there was a determination in her stride.

'Are you John Tisdale's brother?'

Luke stared at the young woman. Her brown eyes were urgent.

'Yes.'

'Can we talk?'

'You'd better come inside,' Eloise said.

Ezra stepped down.

'McPherson, I gotta say one thing,' Curly said after the others went inside the office, and he gripped the reins. 'I didn't know nothing about what happened to that boy today.'

'Nobody said you did.'

'I don't like all this killing.'

'If you hang around, you're going to see more.'

'You're certain of that, ain't you?'

Curly looked at Ezra's face and got his answer. He snapped the reins and the phaeton hurried down the street.

'Well, there you are,' Owen said. 'That must have been some kind of dinner. What kept you so long?'

Owen had walked across the street from the barbershop and stopped in the shadow of the overhang.

'I have two or three hairs on the back of my head that needed trimming. I figured – what better time to get a haircut? Ezra, something seems to be ailing you. What's wrong?'

'We ran into some trouble,' Ezra said. 'And, I'm afraid, we've just run into some more.'

Ezra and Owen walked inside the newspaper office. Sitting in a chair in front of one of the desks, Meta accepted the glass of water that Eloise offered. Marcus also sat, but Luke stood, not far from the young woman.

'Would you gentlemen like some water?' Eloise asked.

Ezra shook his head.

'You knew my brother?' Luke asked.

She set the glass on the desk and breathed deeply.

'Yes, I knew John. He and I were – friends.'

'What is your name?'

'Meta Anderson. My family is from Tennessee. We're farmers.'

'Is there something you want to tell us about John Tisdale?' Owen asked.

'Dr Tisdale, I've heard you intend to take his body back East.'

'That's right,' Luke said.

'He wouldn't want that.'

'What do you mean?'

'He would want to be buried out here,' she said. 'I guess to a lot of people one place is as good as another, but he loved this land. He loved what people like my family are trying to do. I wish I could say I share his love, but I'm not going to lie. Personally, I would prefer to be on an eastbound right this minute. But John looked at Wyoming and saw possibilities. I know he would want to stay here.'

Luke sat in a chair and stared at the floor. Ezra walked up to Meta.

'Ma'am, what else aren't you telling us?'

'I'm telling you enough, ain't I? John wanted to buy a spread.'

'Why would he want to do that? He had a job.'

'He didn't like it.'

Luke raised his head.

'How do you know?'

'He told me. He said he was going to leave Swearingen. He said he couldn't talk much about it, something about Swearingen being a client.'

'Apparently he confided in you quite a bit,' Owen said.

'Meta, how are you going to get home?' Eloise asked.

'I've got Buttercup. That's my mule.'

'Why don't you let somebody take you?'

'No, thank you, ma'am. That won't be necessary. Thank you for the water.'

Meta stood and walked to the door.

'Miss Anderson, wait,' Luke said. 'What did my brother say about Jekyll Island?'

She smiled.

'He had wonderful things to say about Jekyll Island. He told me he didn't get to spend much time there. You know, Swearingen kept him pretty busy. But he told me he loved to hunt quail. He said Mr McPherson taught him how to hunt. He had kind things to say about you, Mr McPherson. One of his fondest memories, he said, was the three of you hunting quail. He said you and the dogs moved as one. I've never seen the ocean. I've never smelled the salt in the air. He told me he would take me there one day. But he said it would just be a visit. Wyoming was home.'

Luke rose from the chair and stood before Meta.

'Miss Anderson, I'm going to bury John tomorrow, tomorrow afternoon. Would he have liked the town cemetery?'

'That would have suited him just fine.'

'I'll have to get a preacher. We should be ready around two o'clock.'

'Luke, are you sure about this?' Ezra asked. 'Do you want to telegraph your father?'

'I'm sure.'

'I'll be there,' Meta said. 'Believe me – this is what your brother would have wanted.'

'I believe you.'

'Miss, I'll walk you across the street,' Ezra said.

Ezra and Meta walked to the livery. They said nothing. She kept her face turned, and he knew she was crying. Smitty had the mule waiting. Meta reached for the leather pouch that hung from her worn leather belt, but Smitty held up his hands.

'No, ma'am. You don't have to pay me a thing.'

'Thank you, Smitty.'

Smitty cupped his hands and helped her on to the mule's back. She looked down at Ezra and smiled and then rode out of the stable. Ezra pulled out a twenty-dollar gold piece.

'I'm going to need a horse later today.'

'Yes, sir. I won't take her money, but I'll take yours.'

'Yeah, I bet you will. Smitty, if you don't mind me asking, but where did you get that limp?'

'Shiloh. Bloodiest fighting I ever saw. You've done your share of fighting. I can tell.'

'I've done enough.'

'Some of Swearingen's men have been asking about you. You oughtta know.'

'I appreciate it. Will twenty dollars get me the use of a good horse?'

'It'll get you the best in the corral.'

'I'll be by later. Thanks, Smitty.'

Ezra walked back to the newspaper office. He glanced at the sidewalk. Standing in the shadows beneath the overhang of the barbershop was the deputy. Apparently he had been keeping an eye on Owen, and now it was time to keep an eye on Ezra. He leaned against a post that supported the overhang, and he watched.

'I know the Methodist minister,' Eloise said.

'We're Presbyterians,' Luke said.

'It's not going to make any difference,' Ezra said, and he closed the door.

'After the funeral, will you head back East?' Marcus asked.

'I don't know,' Luke said.

'You got no need to stay,' Owen said.

'My brother's killer is still loose.'

'You'd better let the sheriff handle it,' Eloise said.

'The lady's right,' Ezra said.

116

'Maybe I'll decide to practise here,' Luke said.

'What about Boston?'

'Boston has plenty of doctors. I'm going to give it some thought.'

Luke left the office and Ezra shook his head.

'Well, old friend,' Owen said, 'things just keep getting complicated.'

CHAPTER 15

Mitch Harrison sat at his desk and studied at the blank sheet of paper. Beside it lay a pencil. I've been looking at this piece of paper for an hour, he said to himself, and I haven't picked up the pencil. Well, it's time I do it. He squinted and adjusted the wire-rimmed glasses perched on his nose and he took up the pencil. He tapped it several times on the desk and then forced it to move on the paper.

Mayor Payne,
Retirement is something I've thought about a long time. I don't like admitting it, but I'm getting old, too old to keep doing what I'm doing.

He pulled a yellowed handkerchief from his trouser pocket and wiped the sweat from his forehead. Retirement. He hated the word. Old. He hated that word too. Maybe I should just write, 'I quit' and be done with it. And, then, what will I do? What does an old man like me who is wifeless and childless do? And what have I accomplished? When I walk out of this office for the last time, what will I be remembered for? Do I really care? Yes, I care. Otherwise, I wouldn't sit here in this damn heat and wonder.

Boots came down heavy on the sidewalk, just outside the door. He opened a drawer and tossed the letter and waited for the door knob to turn. His hand rested on the pistol next to his hip. He didn't have to wait long. A half dozen men – farmers, he could tell, some of whom he had seen going in and out of Taylor's General Store, some of whom had bought lumber from Taylor's lumber yard behind the store – shuffled into the office. He didn't know their names. Their boots scratched the floor and brought dust from the land. Their faces were dark and unshaven. They smelled of sweat.

'You're Sheriff Harrison,' one said.

'I'm not trying to keep it a secret. Who the hell are you and what do you want?'

'My name is Darton. These men are my neighbours. I want – we all want – justice.'

'Well, that makes things as clear as a mudhole after a rain. We all want justice in this world.'

'My oldest boy Cliff was murdered today. He was lynched. My other boy Jody saw it all. He said it was Swearingen's men. What are you going to do about it?'

Harrison removed his spectacles and lay them on the desk. He studied Darton. The man was in pain. For many years he had seen that kind of pain. It was the kind of pain that would outlive any justice that might be served. But right now Darton wasn't thinking about that.

'Mr Darton, I'm sorry to hear about your boy. Indeed, I am. Your son, the one who saw everything, does he know for a fact it was Swearingen's men?'

'He knows. Swearingen's men came to our place the other night. They told us something bad was going to happen if we didn't get out.'

These men had come a long way to homestead in Wyoming, and they weren't going to head back to wherever it was they came from. Harrison had known men like these. He

119

had known them for a long time. He had once been one of them.

'I guess you know that in a court of law it's going to be the word of your son against the word of those men. It's going to be hard to prosecute.'

'Are you saying you ain't going to do anything?' another man said. 'My son Sven was shot down in a saloon just last night by the young Swearingen.'

'Yeah, I heard about it. Plenty of witnesses said it was self-defence.'

'Self-defence? Is that what you call it?'

'That's what the witnesses called it.'

'I bet that gunman who stopped the train robbery would do something.'

'That gunman who stopped the train robbery isn't the sheriff, and I am,' Harrison said. 'Mr Darton, you have my sympathy. It's not the first time a man has been lynched for no reason. But you have to understand – in court it's going to be the word of a boy against men, and you can bet they will all have alibis. Who's the jury going to believe?'

'So what I've been hearing is true,' Darton bit the words one by one. 'You won't do anything.'

'I'll do what the law says I can do.'

'My youngest boy said one of the men was called Andrew. I reckon he's the one who killed Sven Burleson. My son wouldn't have made it up. Maybe the law says you can do something about him. He can't claim self-defence when there's a lynching.'

Damn, Harrison thought.

'I'll ride out to the Swearingen place and ask a few questions. Not tonight. First thing in the morning. I'll look into it, but I can't make any promises.'

The farmers turned and filed through the door. They weren't happy. Harrison could tell by the way they shuffled their feet. He hadn't told them what they wanted to hear. If they thought he would immediately saddle up and ride out to Swearingen's this late in the day, they could just keep on thinking. After the last one left, Stuart came in.

'What was all that about?'

'There's been another killing, a lynching. It seems Andrew Swearingen was involved. Those men want justice. And I can't say I blame them.'

Richard Swearingen sat in the wing chair next to the cold fireplace and lifted the glass of bourbon. The library of the gentlemen's club was dark. Only one dim lamp on the large mantle offered any light. Swearingen did not understand why the room was always so dark. The club had electric lights, but apparently the other three men preferred the darkness. He set the glass on a mahogany table and lit a cigar. The others – Lansing, Palmer, Schultz – sat in their leather chairs and watched.

'Your men are causing some trouble.'

Swearingen stared at Palmer, whose white hair seemed the only thing visible in the darkness.

'My men are not causing trouble,' Swearingen said. 'They are protecting what is mine and, for that matter, what is yours.'

'Lynching a boy is not the proper course of action,' Schultz said.

Like Palmer, Schultz was an old man, and Swearingen wondered why he ever ventured out West. But the lure of money, even for an old man, was strong.

'Lynching – not exactly the word I would use,' Swearingen said. 'It's my understanding this boy, as you call him, had rustled some of my cows. That sort of thing cannot be tolerated. Out here those kinds of transgressions must be dealt with quickly. This is not New York, Mr Schultz.'

'There's talk of a range war.'

'Mr Schultz, you're listening to your ranch hands, and ranch hands tend to engage in hyperbole. But if the homesteaders choose to pursue violence, then my men are prepared to answer accordingly. And, I trust, the same holds true for your men.'

'We seem to forget that once, with the exception of Mr Lansing, we were poor,' Schultz said. 'Why should we be so hard on these homesteaders?'

'Simple economics,' Swearingen said. 'The land is drought-stricken. Without ample pasture, without ample water, our cattle will perish, and so will our investment. I don't begrudge the homesteaders seeking a better life. They just need to seek it somewhere else.'

'Maybe we should bring some Sioux from a reservation and let them do a little rain dance,' Lansing said.

Lansing was young. He too was in finance in New York, and Swearingen saw him as a threat – not today, not tomorrow, but down the road. He had not had to work for his money. His family had owned textile mills in Massachusetts for generations. He had tried to move into the garment industry in New York. Swearingen, with John Tisdale's help, was able to cut him off. He closed the deal. Lansing never mentioned it. Swearingen suspected the defeat festered beneath Lansing's skin. Lansing decided to leave the garment industry behind and to do something different, to be a different Lansing. He came West. Swearingen knew of only one man who was thinner, more emaciated than Rayburn – and it was Lansing. Swearingen had won one battle with him, and he did not trust him – not in New York, not in Wyoming.

'Sometimes I wish I had stayed in New York,' Palmer said.

'Have you forgotten, Mr Palmer,' Swearingen said, 'you were the one who first encouraged me to come out here? And you, Mr Schultz, you had already established quite an enterprise by the time I got out here. Have you forgotten? You helped me get my first herd. Gentlemen, we all came to Wyoming because we knew there was a profit to be made. Let us not lose sight of that. Admittedly, the weather has not been an ally. But adversity is something we can deal with. We have dealt with it countless times before, and we will deal with it countless times in the future. The homesteaders are just another form of adversity, and we must deal with them.'

They sat in the darkness and they smoked and they drank. The room smelled of dark wood and cigars. A rug from Persia lay at their feet, a gift Swearingen had given the club.

'But this killing – I don't like it,' Schultz said.

'What about those miners who were killed?' Swearingen asked. 'They questioned the way you ran your mines. And you wouldn't stand for any strikes.'

'That was different.'

'And how the hell was it different, Mr Schultz? You were protecting what was yours, and that's what we're doing now. If you gentlemen have lost the stomach for this sort of bloody business, then just stand back. I will handle things, I promise you. I have the men to do it.'

'We've put the handling of this situation in your hands,' Lansing said. 'You have assured us that you can produce the desired outcome.'

'And I can.'

'What about the gunfighter on the train?' Palmer asked. 'Can you handle him?'

'I don't know much about him,' Swearingen said. 'But whoever he is, I can handle him.'

'See that you do,' Lansing said. 'See that you do.'

'Well, I've found the conversation most stimulating,' Swearingen said. 'But right now I need something besides conversation to stimulate me, so I must leave the confines of the gentlemen's club for the confines of the sporting club.

Good evening, gentlemen.'

Swearingen grabbed hold of the arms of the chair and pushed himself up. He crossed the rug and slammed the door behind him.

'You know, if I had a wife as attractive as Ginevra Swearingen,' Palmer said, 'I don't think I'd be going to a sporting club. I've seen what they have to offer.'

'I bet you have,' Lansing said.

'I don't like this talk of war,' Schultz said. 'Nothing good can come of it. When the guns start blazing, what's to keep Swearingen from going back to New York and leaving us to deal with the carnage?'

'The gunman on the train,' Lansing said, 'Swearingen is afraid of him. The fear is in his eyes. He doesn't know who he is, so he doesn't know how to deal with him. He doesn't know who he's going up against.'

'Lack of information,' Palmer said, 'is not a good thing – not a good thing at all in a war.'

'He may not have the information he needs,' Lansing said, 'but he has pride. He believes he has established a kingdom on the prairie of Wyoming. He believes he is impervious to any harm. But we know better. Don't we, gentlemen?'

Schultz rose and crossed the floor to the door.

'Where are you off to?' Lansing asked.

Schultz did not answer. He walked down the dark hall and through the large chandelier-lit reception room and through a doorway to the bar. It was empty, except for Burt, the bartender, a man almost as old as Schultz. The panelled walls were black walnut.

'What can I get for you?'

'Whiskey,' Schultz said.

He lifted the glass and drank. The warmth spread quickly. It was what he needed. He was tired of drinking with the others. He had to get away from them. Burt stood several feet away, close enough to be of service, close enough to engage in conversation, but far enough away to let his customer think. A good bartender, Schultz thought.

Next to the mirror behind the bar a portrait of a young lady hung. Her face was round, the cheeks rosy, the curls long and blonde.

'Who is that?' Schultz asked.

'Her name was Eileen Milsaps. She was a singer. She sang here in town a number of years ago. Just a few performances, and then she was gone. She sat for this portrait. The artist – I don't recollect his name. He didn't stay in town very long – finished it after she left. He told me he used a bit of imagination. I don't know what happened to either one of them.'

Schultz stared at the face, the ringlets that framed it, the smile. They looked so familiar, and then he remembered the greyness of the twilight. The gunfire, the shouts, the screams – they were all gone, lost in a stillness he had never felt before. He remembered putting on his coat and walking down the street, mist coating his face. When he turned the corner, he saw them – men lying in the street, at the curb, detectives hovering above them.

'These anarchists won't give you no more trouble, Mr Schultz. But I don't think you oughtta be out here. A few are still roaming about.'

He had walked past the detective, and stopped. A young woman whose threadbare coat was as grey as the twilight sat at the curb beside one of the men. She was cradling his bloody head in her lap. Men rushed past her. Shrill whistles split the air. She had kissed the top of the head in her lap, and then she looked up. Schultz stood only a few feet away. She had said nothing, but her eyes had said everything.

Schultz stared at the portrait, at the eyes, and he remembered.

'Burt, do you ever wish you could stop time, turn it back?'

'Yes, sir. But we just have to keep pushing forward, doing the best we can.'

'So many mistakes. So many.'

'We're just human, Mr Schultz.'

'Yes, we're just human. And we do what we must do to survive. I believe I will have another whiskey.'

CHAPTER 16

Luke gave the message to the telegraph operator, a young man with long, nervous, slender fingers.

'Send that right away,' Luke said.

'Yes, sir, you bet.'

Luke turned to Marcus and Owen.

'Well, that's done. Father won't be too happy, but Meta Anderson convinced me that burying John here is the right thing to do.'

'You have to do what you think is right,' Marcus said.

'Are you gents ready for some supper?' Owen asked. 'My stomach is growling.'

'You two go ahead,' Luke said. 'I want to go for a walk.'

Marcus and Owen left the telegraph office at the train depot and headed toward the hotel to find Ezra.

'Well, he's saving us a trip upstairs,' Owen said.

Ezra walked out the door and came down the steps. Bright lights burst from the saloon windows into the dusk. A young man on a bicycle rolled past.

'Look at the size of that front wheel,' Owen said. 'I need one of them contraptions.'

'You couldn't keep your balance,' Ezra said.

'Ezra, are you going somewhere?' Marcus asked.

'Yeah, are you going somewhere?' Owen said. 'You've had

a bath. I don't see any dust on you. Of course, I haven't checked behind your ears. You've got a clean shave.'

'And your suit is freshly pressed,' Marcus said.

'Both of you are awfully observant,' Ezra said. 'Is there a law against a man getting a bath, a shave, and a pressed suit?'

'What are you doing with spurs on?' Owen said. 'Planning to take an evening ride?'

'What if I am?'

'It is a nice evening for a ride, though a might hot,' Owen said. 'Want some company?'

'Can't say I do.'

Ezra tipped his wide-brimmed black hat and walked toward the livery at the end of the street. Owen called after him, and he stopped.

'You watch yourself, Ezra. Remember where your home is. And it's not Wyoming.'

'Maybe he wants Wyoming to be his home,' Marcus said. 'It's beautiful country. A man could do worse.'

'Ezra's not just any man. He can't stay here. He has to return to Jekyll Island. Marcus, there are just some things you don't know about Ezra.'

'I'm trying to find out. You can tell me.'

'So you can write an article in your newspaper.'

'That's what I'm paid to do.'

Eloise walked up the sidewalk. She wore a dark green silk dress, and Marcus said to himself that she simply did not look like a newspaper editor.

'Did I hear someone mention the word newspaper?' she asked.

'I don't believe Owen appreciates my line of work,' Marcus said.

'Shame on you, Mr Chesterfield. I thought I saw Ezra heading for the livery.'

'He wants to go for an evening ride,' Owen said.

128

'I see. Well, would you gentlemen like to buy a lady dinner?'

Hoofbeats came up the hill and Ginevra turned. Her mare whinnied.

'It's all right, girl.'

Ezra climbed down from the saddle and tied the stallion to a low-hanging cottonwood branch. He walked to her and removed his hat.

'Hearing your spurs brings back memories,' she said. 'You know, Pa always said he could identify a man by the sound of his spurs. He didn't have to see him. All he had to do was to hear his spurs.'

'Your pa was a smart man. I don't think he ever liked me. He didn't think I'd ever amount to much. Like I said, he was a smart man.'

'I don't think he ever liked any man who came around.'

Below them the Medicine Bow River flowed slowly across the prairie and glimmered in the starlight. In the distance, above the dark peaks of the mountains, jagged shards of lightning split open the sky.

'Lightning,' Ginevra said, 'and not a drop of rain. I've never liked dry-weather lightning. It's ominous. It portends something that's not good.'

They sat on the crest and stared at the river.

'I understand why you like to come here,' he said. 'This is a beautiful spot.'

'I don't even know whether this hill belongs to my husband. I'm sure it does. He owns so much of this land.'

She breathed softly. The sweetness of her perfume was different. It had a richness about it. It was not what he remembered.

'I never expected to find you here in Wyoming,' he said.

'Rest assured, Ezra McPherson, I never expected to find

you in my house.'

He reclined on an elbow but did not look at her.

'It's interesting how things work out – and how they don't work out.'

'Yes, it certainly is. Ezra, why have you come to Cheyenne?'

'Luke intended to take his brother's body East. I'm just here to help, to look after Luke. He tends to get a little hot-headed now and then. But things have changed. It looks like John will be buried here.'

'I suppose he would have liked that.'

'How well did you know him?'

She hesitated. Lightning broke open the sky again, and she trembled. He touched her hand.

'It's far away. It won't touch us.'

'I didn't know him well. Occasionally he would come to see Richard. They would go into the study. The last time he came – they argued. I was upstairs, but I could hear their voices. I couldn't tell what they were saying, but it sounded as if they weren't too happy. Of course, Richard has a way of making people unhappy. He has a special gift.'

Ezra pulled a cigarette from his shirt pocket.

'You mind?'

'No.'

He struck a match and her face shone pale in the sudden light.

'Gin, I'm sorry things haven't worked out the way you hoped. I truly am.'

'Oh, don't feel sorry for me. Peter has a wonderful wife and they're about to have a baby. My youngest, Andrew, is the one I'm concerned about.'

'And you should be. Your youngest is about to get himself in big trouble.'

'Please don't say that. Despite everything, he's still my baby.'

'There was a lynching today – someone else's baby. And your baby apparently was involved.'

She lowered her head and tried to fight back tears. She didn't want Ezra to see her cry.

'Our foreman – a man named Rayburn – is leading him down a violent path.'

'Talk to your son,' Ezra said. 'Tell him he has to leave. If the sheriff is any good, he'll come for your boy. Your husband may not be able to protect him.'

Ezra drew a deep puff on the cigarette and released the smoke, faint white in the summer darkness. Crickets sang and along the river's edge a bullfrog bellowed. For a moment he felt as he did as a boy, when he and Ginevra would sit on the cool river bank in twilight, but the moment did not last. Riders, a half dozen of them, hurried across the prairie on the far side of the river.

'I wonder what sort of mischief those boys are up to,' Ezra said.

'You used to ride at night.'

He lay on his back and stared at the stars. There must be a million of them, he thought.

'That was a long time ago.'

'And now Jesse is dead.'

'Yes. Jesse's dead.'

'I was always afraid you'd be killed,' she said. 'Jesse was crazy. Frank had a level head on his shoulders, but Jesse was crazy. I was so afraid he would drag you into something that would cost you your life. I begged you to run away with me to New York. I knew you'd be safe there.'

'Well, I reckon I ran away. At least that's what Jesse said I was doing. Running away.'

'The years passed, and then I heard what I had feared. I heard you were probably dead. No one knew where you were. So everybody just assumed you were dead. Probably ambushed alongside a forgotten road. The day I heard – I cried. I cried all afternoon. My dear husband noticed. He didn't even ask what the matter was. He had a big deal working – some railroad business. I don't guess he could be bothered.'

'Why did you go to New York?'

'I loved singing. Don't you remember? I wanted to sing on the stage, and I thought I would get the opportunity in New York. I was in a chorus in a theatre that didn't look much better than the barn on Pa's farm. Right after the war Richard came to one of the shows. He took an interest in me. Even though the war was hardly over, he was starting to do well in finance, so I took an interest in him. I guess he thought having a singer for a wife might open some of society's doors to him, and I thought the same thing about him. We were both wrong.'

'But you have money. I would think New York society would welcome both of you with open arms.'

'You don't know New York society. You see, Richard had to work for his money. And I certainly didn't start out with money. So some doors are forever closed. It galls Richard. It's what you used to call a burr in his saddle. But enough of me. There's a question I've been turning over in my mind again and again. So now I'll ask it. Why did you leave Jesse and Frank?'

'The war was over. I had seen enough killing. It was simply time – to go home.'

'That wasn't what you said in '64. Do you remember?'

'Yes, I remember.'

'I was so surprised to see you ride up. It was a cold, rainy November evening. You were soaked. You said you just had to see me again.'

'That was the truth.'

'I thought you had had enough of war. I thought you were home for good.'

'I should have stayed home. When Atlanta fell, we pretty much were finished.'

'And you said that even though the South was going to lose, you and Jesse and Frank and some other Missouri boys were going to make it hard on the Yankees. The Confederate army might surrender, but you never would. Do you remember?'

'Yes, I remember.'

'And then first thing the next morning, in the cold mist, you saddled your horse and rode away. I knew then I couldn't stay. I packed a bag and headed for New York.'

'When I got home after the war ended and found out you were gone, well, it was the worst day of my life. I thought I would never see you again.'

'But the banks – the trains. . . .'

'Yeah, we made it hard on anybody that didn't sympathize with the Confederacy.'

'Eventually you had enough.'

'And I walked away.'

'And Jesse didn't take it well.'

Ezra stared into the darkness. He saw the small cabin. No lamp burned. The chill of late spring filled the room, but no fire burned in the fireplace. Ezra saw it again.

'He called me a coward,' Ezra said.

'After all that you'd done?'

'As far as Jesse was concerned, what we were doing – robbing the banks, the trains – it was no longer about the South. It was all about him. He seemed to take some pleasure out of killing a man. When I told him I was leaving, he went for his gun. Before it cleared the holster, I held mine pointed right between his eyes. He said, "Go ahead, Ezra. I don't think you will."

'Frank told him to shut up. I didn't say anything. And suddenly Jesse just started laughing. I'll never forget it. I just

133

backed out of the room, keeping my gun fixed on him. If I had pulled the trigger, Bob Ford would have never become such a celebrity.'

He sat up and with creaking bones stood. He walked to the edge of the crest. Across the river the riders had disappeared. He felt her standing beside him.

'How did you end up on Jekyll Island?'

'One day a man rode out to the farm,' he said. 'It was six years ago. Ford had killed Jesse just a few days before. One thing that still stands out clear as day in my memory is how well dressed this fellow was. He wore a nice plaid suit, white shirt, tie. He looked like a greenhorn. But he didn't ride like a greenhorn. He looked like he knew what he was doing on a horse. I was slopping the hogs, and he got off his horse and walked over. "The name's Owen Chesterfield", he said. "Am I supposed to be impressed?" I asked. That made him laugh. Of course, I later learned, it didn't take a whole lot to make Owen Chesterfield laugh. He said he was a Pinkerton. Well, that got my attention real fast. I wasn't wearing a gun, so I figured I was in trouble. He sensed it. "Don't worry", he said. "I'm not here to arrest you, though that's what I should do. Let's go inside and talk. I never like discussing business in front of hogs".

'We went inside and sat at the table. Ma always kept the place looking neat and clean. I had just let things go. Dirty clothes lying all over the floor. I made a pot of coffee and we sat at the table and shot the breeze. We talked about the weather. We talked a little politics. He said it was too bad about Jesse. I asked if he had anything to do with it. He said no, and I believed him. I still do.

' "Have you ever wanted a new life?" Owen asked. "Not too many folks get a chance to have a new life. But, Ezra, that's why I'm here. I'm here to offer you a new life".'

'A new life?' Ginevra asked.

'That's what he said. He said he knew I had ridden with Jesse and Frank. I told him I gave all that up years ago. I hadn't even seen Jesse and Frank in a long time. "Folks will put pressure on you to take Jesse's place," he said. "The bloodshed isn't going to stop. You've been a part of it. If you stay here, it'll pull you back in. You need to leave, start fresh. I can give you that new life. We do not want a resumption of the bank and train robbing you were once a part of. The governor doesn't really care what you did in the past. He just doesn't want you doing something in the future we'll all regret".

'He reached into his coat pocket and pulled out a train ticket and gave it to me. It's funny. I was more used to robbing trains than riding on them.'

'What made you decide to accept his offer?'

'What was left for me in Missouri? Just a worn-out farm. Ma and Pa were both dead. Four brothers were killed in the war. One went missing, and I still don't know what happened to him. And you were gone. There was nothing to keep me in Missouri. Owen made arrangements for me to work for Everett Tisdale in Pennsylvania. I had never heard of the man, but I found out he owned a steel company in Pittsburgh. He and Carnegie were big rivals. Can you see me in a place like Pittsburgh? I didn't exactly fit in. It was like pulling a catfish off a river bottom and telling it it was going to live on dry land. Fortunately Tisdale bought a place on Jekyll Island, and I went there. He needed someone who could teach his rich friends how to hunt and shoot. That was something I knew how to do.'

Ezra flung the cigarette down and crushed it beneath his boot.

'I met a young woman today who reminded me a lot of you,' he said. 'She wants to get away from this country.'

'The promised land. Some search for it in the West, some

135

in the East. We have such dreams. Have you found your dream on Jekyll Island?'

'It's beautiful. There's nothing like standing on a sand dune, the sea oats waving in the salty air, and the waves roaring, and the wind blowing.'

'Do you think I would like Jekyll?'

He wrapped his arm around her. Beyond the black mountains lightning flashed across the sky. She pulled back.

'After Luke Tisdale buries his brother,' she said, 'get on the eastbound train. Forget we ever saw each other again.'

'I don't know that I can leave. These homesteaders need help.'

'Ezra, I know the kind of help you're talking about. It can get you killed. My husband can be – ruthless. His foreman is a killer. I can see it in his eyes. The word is that he was involved in the hunt for Jesse and Frank. For all I know, he may be the one who promised Ford glory and riches if he killed Jesse.'

'Yeah, I've heard about him.'

'Let the homesteaders take care of themselves.'

He pulled her back close and bent his head toward hers. He hesitated, and then his lips found hers. The kiss took them both back to hot Missouri nights when she slipped out of her farmhouse and they ran to the river and held each other in the darkness and she told him her father would kill him if he found them.

Those Missouri nights were gone, only something to be remembered. He wiped away tears that shimmered beneath her eyes.

'I'll always love you, Gin.'

'Don't say that. Don't waste your love on me.'

'I can't change how I feel – even after all these years. I should have never lost you. Losing you meant I lost myself.'

'But you found yourself again on Jekyll Island. That's

where you belong. You must return there. If you stay here, you may be killed.'

'These people – these homesteaders – I can't turn my back on them. I can't run away.'

'It's not your job to. . . .'

'If I don't help them, who will?'

'I love you, Ezra. I don't want you to be killed.'

He walked to his horse and rode down the hill. She remained on the hilltop, and lightning streaked across the sky.

CHAPTER 17

Meta sat on the ripped, faded couch. Her father towered over her. He held his large hardened hands, palms up, toward her.

'Why did you go see Tisdale's brother?' Jeremy Anderson asked. 'Can you please explain why?'

Meta looked up at her father's sunburned face. All day he had worked in the pasture putting up a fence. In the darkness barely touched by the lamp on the table, she could see that his shirt was soaked with sweat. She saw the exasperation. Her mother seemed helpless, and Meta felt ill. She wanted to run out the door and never look back.

'It was something I had to do.'

'Involving ourselves with the Tisdales is the last thing we should be doing,' he said. 'Don't you realize we're on the verge of a war?'

'I don't know about those things. All I know is John would have wanted to be buried here, not back East, and I told his brother. There's nothing wrong with that.'

'I should have never let John Tisdale come around. Never. It was against my better judgment. He was close to Swearingen, and Swearingen is our enemy. He wants us out of Wyoming, and this is our home. We're not leaving.'

'John was a good boy,' Isabelle said. 'He was not like Swearingen.'

'We don't know what he was like.'

'I do,' Meta said. 'And Ma's right. He was a good man. He was going to leave Swearingen, and Swearingen had him murdered.'

'You don't know that. You shouldn't be saying things you don't know. Outside these four walls, don't say things like that.'

He was afraid. Meta knew. She stood and faced him. He wore dust-covered overalls. He smelled of sweat. He clasped his hands behind him.

'Yes, I know it,' he said. 'We all know it. John was good, and Swearingen won't tolerate any good around him.'

Anderson walked to the table and thrust his hands out and grabbed hold of the back of a straight chair.

'They're going to bury John tomorrow at two in the city cemetery,' Meta said. 'I'll be there.'

'No, I don't want you to go.'

'I'm going, Pa. And I want you and Ma to go with me. But whether you do or you don't, I will be there.'

'Jeremy, we should go,' Isabelle said. 'We should pay our respects.'

He looked over his shoulder and nodded his head. The door opened. His eldest son, Asa, stood at the threshold.

'Pa, you'd better come.'

Anderson stood on the porch and stared at the hills. A small spot of redness rose in the distant sky and became pink.

'Isn't that the Davis place?' another son, Cash, said.

'How can you tell?' the youngest son, Alex, asked.

The three brothers held Winchester rifles.

'Yes, it's the Davis place,' Anderson said.

Isabelle and Meta joined him on the porch.

'Do you think I should ride over?' Asa asked.

'No. We can't do them any good. We need to stay here.'

'You don't think the Sioux have come back?' Isabelle asked.

139

'It's not the Sioux. That I can promise you. Asa, I want you and Cash to stay in the barn tonight and keep a lookout. One of you get in the loft. Keep your rifles with you. Alex, you stay here in the house. We'll take turns sitting up. If any of you hear or see anything, let me know right away.'

Anderson went inside and closed the door. Meta stared at the fiery red cloud. It was so far away, yet she knew it was violent, all-consuming. The Davis family seemed like nice folks. Their dream was burning, twisting in a red spiral into the blackness of the Wyoming sky, and she wondered if they were alive or dead.

Luke walked past the small wood one- and two-storey homes that lined both sides of the wide street. Most had front porches. With light easing out the windows, the row of homes held a sense of comfort, something he hadn't felt in a long time. The smell of supper was in the nighttime air, and the smell was good.

Tomorrow his brother would be buried. And then he would probably board the Union Pacific for his return East. But was that really what he wanted to do? Ezra would insist. Owen would concur. And Marcus? Well, he would just observe and perhaps write about it.

'Dr Tisdale, is that you?'

Luke stopped in front of a house. A dark figure rose from the porch swing and came to the steps.

'Yes.'

She walked to the fence gate and smiled, and he removed his derby.

'Are you taking your evening constitutional?'

'Sometimes it's the only way I can think.'

'Have you had supper?'

'No – I – I haven't even thought about it.'

'Well, there's no need to think about it. We have plenty of

fried chicken left.'

'Your sister and brother-in-law. . . .'

'I assure you they won't mind.'

He followed her inside the house. Silas sat on the couch and held the latest edition of Eloise Endicott's newspaper. Bobby sat on the floor and played with a train he had carved from small chunks of wood. It didn't really look like a train, but he didn't care. It was close enough. It didn't have any wheels, except in his mind.

'Hey, Doctor,' Bobby said. 'You like my train? I carved it myself.'

'You did an outstanding job.'

'Dr Tisdale, this is my brother-in-law, Silas Taylor.'

Silas stood and the two men shook hands. Charlotte came in from the kitchen.

'Charlotte, you remember Dr Tisdale?'

'I certainly do. Welcome.'

'It turns out Dr Tisdale hasn't had supper,' Jennifer said.

'We'll take care of that,' Charlotte said. 'The dining room is this way.'

'Yes, please come in and eat,' Silas said.

Luke sat at the table and soon a plate of fried chicken, biscuits and brown gravy was before him. Silas started to sit, but Charlotte pushed him toward the living room.

'We should let Dr Tisdale eat in peace,' Charlotte said. 'Bobby, you come too.'

Jennifer brought two cups of coffee and sat.

'The chicken is wonderful,' Luke said. 'I haven't had any good fried chicken in a long time.'

'Charlotte is a divine cook. There's also apple cobbler.'

'I mustn't impose.'

'I insist.'

After the meal, Jennifer poured more coffee and they took their cups to the front porch. Silas continued to read the paper, Charlotte worked with her crocheting, and Bobby dragged his train on the floor in front of the fireplace. Luke and Jennifer sat in the swing. The night was quiet. No music from the saloons found its way into the neighbourhood.

'Are you about ready to take your brother back East?' she asked.

'I'm not taking him back East.'

'I don't understand.'

'Things have changed. John is going to be buried here, here in Cheyenne. A young lady who knew him came to see me today. She said John would have wanted to be buried here. I think she knew him well. I believed her.'

'Will there be a funeral?'

'Yes. Two o'clock tomorrow.'

'I would like to come.'

'I appreciate it, but you don't have to.'

'I know I don't have to. I want to.'

He realized her feet did not quite touch the floor. He had not intended to come to this house. Earlier that day he had not intended to walk to the schoolhouse. Somehow his feet just kept leading him to this young woman with beautiful, long blonde hair and a soft Southern voice. Now he sat in the darkness beside her. Returning to the East was something he did not desire. Remaining in Cheyenne seemed a real possibility, and he knew his father would never understand.

'I've taken too much of your time today,' he said. 'First, this morning. And now.'

'Dr Tisdale, do you hear me complaining?'

'You should call me Luke. I'd be much obliged if you called me that.'

'All right. And I have a name besides Mrs Beauchamp. It's Jennifer.'

He took her hand and held it. It was small and warm and

142

he did not want to let it go. But he knew he should return to town. Ezra would be searching for him. And then again maybe not. Ezra was acting strange. Somehow the journey to the Swearingen ranch had had some effect on him.

'I must be going,' he said. 'Thank you for the meal. It was delicious. Please tell your sister and brother-in-law how much I appreciate their hospitality.'

They stood and walked to the gate.

'I'll see you tomorrow,' she said.

He walked along the street. A freshness hung in the air, the kind that followed a rain, yet there had been no rain. It was as if the freshness that clung to Jennifer followed him, as if the warmth of her hand still touched his hand. Suddenly he stopped.

'What am I doing?' he asked aloud.

He knew the answer. He closed his eyes and he saw her face. He hardly knew her, yet it seemed he had known her a long time.

'Well, I guess I'll be sending Father another telegram.'

He walked past Slade's. The windows were dark. Inside lay the body of his brother.

'Not much longer, John, not much longer.'

'Who you talking to, son?'

Startled and embarrassed, Luke turned. A man in a dark suit left a one-storey building and crossed the street. He was not tall, but he was wide, and Luke could not help grinning. He suspected the fellow was no stranger to biscuits and gravy. The man pushed his hat back. Luke saw that he was not young. In the dim streetlight his beard glowed white.

'You're the young doctor from back East,' he said. 'Somebody pointed you out to me when you were walking down the street. I'm Sam Grierson. When folks need a doctor, they generally come see me.'

'Dr Grierson, I'm pleased to meet you.'

They shook hands. Luke smelled whiskey on the old man's breath.

'I'm sorry about your brother. I wish I could have done something. He was dead by the time I got to him.'

'We're going to bury him tomorrow – here in Cheyenne.'

'After that?'

'I don't know. I had planned to go back East.'

'But you may change your mind. You're thinking about staying.'

'I wouldn't want to trespass on your practice.'

'Nonsense. I'd welcome you. I'm an old man. I can't journey all over creation like I once could. Besides, I drink too much. If I don't tell you, somebody else will. If you need your left leg cut off, I just might cut off the right.'

'I'm sure that's comforting news to your patients.'

'They get what they pay for, and most of them don't pay a plug nickel. I have to tell you – if you do open up your practice here, you're probably going to have plenty of business, whether they pay or not. There's trouble in the air. I've lived in the West a long time. I know when the storm clouds are building up. A range war is brewing. I've seen it before. Just be prepared.'

'Can you ever be prepared for that sort of thing?'

'Hell no. But be prepared anyway. Got to run, my boy.'

The old doctor staggered into the darkness. And then Luke realized the piano music coming from the saloons was strangely quiet. In fact, the whole street was quiet, deserted. He looked again at Slade's and headed toward the hotel.

Marcus, Owen and Eloise ate dinner at Delmonico's. Owen contributed little to the conversation. His mind was elsewhere. He wondered what Ezra was doing, and he was concerned. Marcus and Eloise noticed. They wanted to ask questions, but they chose to wait. After dinner they walked to the newspaper office.

'Things are not too lively tonight,' Marcus said. 'Even the restaurant was quiet.'

'Compared to the way it usually is, Cheyenne is a ghost town tonight,' Eloise said. 'Marcus, you don't think Luke is into any mischief, do you? I'd hate for him to be a headline in my paper tomorrow.'

'I'd hate that too.'

'And I'd hate for Ezra to be a headline. Wouldn't you, Owen?'

'I wouldn't care for it, ma'am,' Owen said.

A cyclist rolled past them. Marcus stared and shook his head.

'Eloise, have you tried riding one of those things?' Marcus asked.

'No. I don't intend to. I have no desire to break my neck.'

They stood outside the newspaper, and a breeze stirred. It was gentle, hardly noticeable, yet still comforting after the heat of the day.

'Gentlemen, a meal like the one we just had deserves a good cup of coffee. Come in and I'll take care of it.'

'Let me,' Owen said. 'Just show me where the pot is and I'll take care of it. You two can sit and talk. You haven't tasted coffee until you've tasted coffee prepared by a Pinkerton.'

'I have a sense of foreboding,' Marcus said.

'Since we're in the presence of a lady, I won't tell you where you can go, but I think you know.'

Marcus and Eloise sat in the dim light of the newspaper office and Owen headed for the wood-burning stove in the back room. The piano in one of the saloons sounded a few notes, first slow, then quick, and grew silent.

'Marcus, I want you to tell me about how you met Ezra, how you ended up here,' she said.

He removed his hat and leaned back in the straight chair

145

so that it touched the wall.

'I've never been able to resist the pull of mystery. I see it and I follow it. I study it and try to learn about it. Ezra is that kind of mystery.'

'What made you go to Jekyll Island in the first place?' she asked. 'I'm not writing an article. I just want to know.'

CHAPTER 18

'I've always liked being in a newspaper late at night when there's nothing but blackness outside the windows and when the rush of the presses retreats into silence. So it was several months ago. It was well past midnight. Everyone had left and I sat at my desk. But Stanley Wilcox was there. He is always there. He is my editor and I don't think he ever leaves the building. At least it doesn't seem like it.

'He came out of his office and headed straight toward me. I figured I had done something he didn't like. He's not the easiest editor to please. Both he and I had worked in Rome, and Henry Grady persuaded us to come to Atlanta. The city is vibrant. You walk down any street and you see buildings going up. Growth – you'd have to say Atlanta and Cheyenne have that in common.

' "Let's go get a drink," Wilcox said. "We need to talk."

'Wilcox seemed friendly, at least as close to friendly as he ever gets. I grabbed my hat and coat and we headed down Marietta Street to Five Points and then to the Kimball House. I don't know if you've ever heard of the Kimball House, but it's quite a hotel. The first one burned. But that's how it is in Atlanta. If something burns, it gets rebuilt. The Kimball House has a bar that stays open late, and Wilcox and I sat at a table and ordered bourbons. He had me curious.

' "Ever heard of Jekyll Island?" he said, and I told him I had. "Well, it's becoming a playground for the rich. I'm talking about the richest of the rich. They're building cottages on the island. I think our readers would like to know what's going on."

' "So you want me to go to Jekyll Island?" I said.

'The idea appealed to me. I had never seen the ocean.

' "Yes. I've been in touch with Everett Tisdale. You know the name? He's from Pittsburgh, owns the Tisdale Steel Works. He also owns a railroad or two. He has a place on Jekyll. He said he'd be happy to have you come. Of course, you have to take your nice manners with you."

' "I wasn't aware I had any."

' "I can see a story here," Wilcox said. "Folks are curious about the rich. And now we have the rich practically in our back yard. I wouldn't give this assignment to just anyone."

' "In other words, the other reporters are working on more important things."

' "Yeah, something like that."

'I rode a train east to Savannah and south to Brunswick. From there I got an old man and his grandson to ferry me across to the island. Night had already settled in. The wind was blowing. Salt spray hit me in the face.

' "Who you going to visit?" the old man asked, and I told him Tisdale. I told him I was a newspaper reporter, and my readers wanted to know all about the rich people on the Georgia coast.

'The old man laughed. I didn't understand.

' "You can talk to all the rich people you want," he said. "But if they're all you talk to, you've come a long way just to waste your time. The man you should talk to ain't rich, but I think your readers would want to know about him."

' "Who is this man?" I said.

' "His name is Ezra McPherson."

' "What's special about him?"

' "Well, sir, I don't know where he came from. But I can tell you this – he sure knows how to handle a gun. That's what he does for Tisdale. He teaches folks how to shoot, how to hunt."

'They took me to the dock and pointed the way to the Tisdale place. I have to confess that I really wasn't looking forward to meeting Everett Tisdale. I had read about him, about the strike at one of his railroads. Troops were brought in. A lot of heads were cracked. A few men were killed. Tisdale broke the strike. He just didn't seem like the kind of man I wanted to meet, but I had a job to do.

'Stanley Wilcox told me that the houses built on Jekyll were cottages. When I went up the long drive between rows of palm trees – and I had never seen a palm tree before – I could tell even in the darkness that the home rising before me was not exactly what I thought of as a cottage. It was large, two-storey. The light coming out the front windows was faint, so I figured the family was probably in the back of the house.

'Before I climbed the steps, I stopped and listened. The roar of the waves came from beyond what I would be told were dunes. It was a moment I'll always remember – the first time I heard the ocean.

'A well-dressed butler let me in and took my hat. He led me down a long hall to a room with a billiard table. A small, thin, silver-haired man lay down his cue and took my hand. His smile was friendly. This man was Everett Tisdale, and he looked nothing like the man I expected, the man who would bring troops in to quell a strike.

' "Marcus, we've been expecting you. This is my son, Luke. Have you eaten? You must be hungry."

'I told him I had eaten on the train. Luke was just as friendly as his father. I found out he was a doctor living in Boston, but he was on Jekyll for most of the summer.

' "Jekyll is a paradise," Tisdale said. "I wish I could have kept it a secret, but something this beautiful just cannot be kept a secret. I love Pittsburgh. It's been home for many years, but the winters – well, they're pretty awful. I've decided to make Jekyll my permanent home. I can return to Pittsburgh when I need to, to make sure the steel is still being produced the way I want it produced. But Jekyll is home now. Tomorrow Luke will show you around the island."

' "I've been told an interesting fellow works here," I said. "I'd sure like to talk to him. His name is Ezra McPherson."

'The old man got this funny look on his face, as if I'd brought up a subject that should have remained under wraps.

' "Well, certainly, Marcus," he said. "I think that can be arranged. But I have to tell you – Mr McPherson is not a talkative sort. Don't be surprised if he has little to say."

'The next day Luke and I rode on chestnut mares around the island. The Spanish moss that hung from the live oaks was beautiful, but also ghostly. We rode on the beach, past children building castles, complete with moats, in the sand. The children came from wealthy families that had already built on the island. The ocean spread out before us and glistened in the sun. We rode inland, past cottages – mansions – under construction. Workers hammered and sawed and wiped sweat and balanced themselves on scaffolding. Luke pointed out which families owned which houses. The families came from New York primarily, but some came from Chicago and Boston.

' "I've been told Jekyll is the summer playground of America's wealthy," I said.

' "It's a wonderful place to come to," Luke said. "I really don't think about the money aspect of things. I guess when your family has it, you just don't think about it that much. And if you don't have it, you think about it a lot."

'We returned to the beach and left our horses and stood on one of the dunes. The wind was brisk, salty.

' "Do you have any brothers or sisters?" I asked.

' "One brother. John is a lawyer. He works for a financier, a man named Swearingen. Right now he's out West, in Cheyenne. Swearingen owns a cattle ranch. He likes to dabble in a lot of things apparently. I haven't seen John in quite a while. He's supposed to come here later this summer."

' "This fellow McPherson – exactly what does he do?"

' "My father entertains a number of business associates on Jekyll. They come by train and by boat. Ezra runs the hunting preserve. My father believes it is easier to conduct business if everyone is relaxed. In other words, it's easier for him to get his way, but don't tell him I said that, and don't print it. Some of these men have never fired a rifle or a shotgun. Ezra teaches them how to shoot. And it's not just the men. He teaches the wives too. He takes them on quail and deer hunts in the winter. You should see the way the bird dogs respond to Ezra in the field. He has a real gift."

' "Where is Mr McPherson from?"

' "From the West. I can't tell you too much about him."

' "Luke, it sounds as if you're not supposed to tell too much about him. It sounds as if mystery surrounds him. Let me guess. He's a wanted outlaw. He's hiding here on Jekyll Island, where no one will think to look for him."

' "You like to read the dime novels about the West, don't you?"

' "I'm afraid I do."

' "Ezra will be at dinner tonight. You'll get to talk to him."

'One thing I learned that day as Luke and I rode across the island was that it was not just a place of relaxation – and of course it was – but it was also a place of business. Tisdale and his cronies conducted business on the island. They could get away from the distractions of New York. They could get away from the ever-watchful eye of the newspapers. They could conduct the nation's business and, at the same time, have a good time on the sandy shores of Jekyll.

'Dinner at the Tisdale cottage was a casual affair, consistent with the theme of relaxation that the old man tried to cultivate. Nevertheless, the table in the dining room was large. Silver adorned a massive sideboard. Servants made certain we wanted nothing. The beef was superb. That I remember. But what I was most interested in was a conversation with the man who sat across from me. Ezra McPherson himself. I suppose it was good that the dress was not formal. Somehow I suspected Ezra had never worn a tie. I had no concrete evidence to support this supposition, just a gut feeling.

'His hair was long, just as it is now. The sun had baked his face. His eyes were the blackest eyes I had ever seen.

' "Ezra, Mr Stokesbury writes for the *Atlanta Constitution*," Tisdale said.

' "You're a long way from home," Ezra said.

' "And how about you, Mr McPherson?" I said. "Are you a long way from home?"

' "I guess that depends on how fast the horse is."

' "Or the train," Tisdale said."Marcus, I'm thinking about investing in railroads right here in Georgia."

' "We could use more railroads," I said. "Mr McPherson, I hear you're good with a gun."

' "I just aim and squeeze the trigger. Not much to it."

' "There's a bit more to it than that," Luke said.

' "Yes, I believe there is," I said.

' "Marcus, you'll have to come back at Christmas," Tisdale said. "We'll have the place decorated. And Ezra can take you on a quail hunt."

' "Yes, we can wager who has the best luck," Luke said. "Of course, Ezra, you can't participate in the wager."

'Before we finished dinner, the butler walked in. He was elderly, older than Tisdale. He had an air of efficiency about him. I had noticed the stoic expression on his face never changed. Only, this time it was different. He carried a small piece of paper, and he handed it to Tisdale.

' "Sir, this is for you."

'Tisdale took the paper and read. His face grew pale, almost as white as his white hair.

' "Father, what is it?" Luke asked.

'The old man handed him the paper. Luke read and shook his head.

' "No, it can't be."

' "Mr Tisdale, what's the matter?" Ezra asked. "Is there something I can do?"

' "John is dead," Tisdale said. "He's been shot, murdered in Cheyenne."

'We were shaken. All I knew about John Tisdale was what Luke had told me, and he hadn't told me much. Still, I felt as if I knew him. Luke bowed his head.

' "I was looking forward so much to his being here this summer," he said.

'Ezra stood and walked to Luke and took the paper and read.

' "I never wanted him to go out there with Swearingen," Tisdale said. "I never had a good feeling about it. John just laughed. "The West isn't what it used to be," he said. "The days of outlaws and gunfights are over. Men like Wyatt Earp have put an end to all that. I'll be fine. Don't worry."

' "I need to go out there and bring him back," Luke said.

' "No, I don't want you to go."

' "I have to go. He's my brother. He would do the same for me."

' "No, Luke. I insist. I've lost one son out there. I can't bear the thought. . . ."

' "I have to go. I'll leave tomorrow."

'Luke rose and walked out of the room. Ezra laid the paper on the table.

' "I'll go with him," Ezra said.

' "Ezra, you can't go," Tisdale said."You know that. You know the agreement. You have to stay here."

' "I'm well aware of the agreement. But somebody has to look after Luke. He doesn't know the West, and I do. I'll make sure nothing happens to him."

'Tisdale nodded his head, and Ezra walked out.

' "Mr Tisdale, I'm awfully sorry," I said."Is there anything I can do?"

' "No, Marcus, but thank you. I just want to be alone."

'I laid my white linen napkin on the table and left the dining room. I stood on the veranda and listened to the crash of the waves and decided to go down to the beach. It was a warm evening. The breeze was brisk, just as brisk as it was earlier in the day. I went past the dunes that stood white in the moonlight. On the shore stood Ezra and Luke.

' "I'm sorry," I said."I wasn't following you. I just thought I'd come here to the beach."

' "That's all right," Luke said."Ezra is still trying to convince me to stay here. What's your opinion?"

' "I should not inject my opinion, Luke. But if you and Mr McPherson are going to Cheyenne, I'd like to come along."

' "You're a newspaperman, all right," Ezra said."You sense a story. Everybody would be better off if you stay here."

' "Ezra, you're not being hospitable. Marcus is Father's guest."

' "He's not my guest."

' "You work for Father. Father's guest is your guest."

' "Well, if you're hell-bent on going, I've got some packing to do," Ezra said.

' "Marcus, you'd be welcome to come along."

'Luke returned to the house and I caught up with Ezra before he entered his cabin not far from the barn. It was a small cabin with tabby walls. You could run your hand over the walls and feel the hard shells. You won't see that kind of wall in Cheyenne. I certainly never saw it in Atlanta. I've been told you find it only along the coast.

' "Mr McPherson, may I ask you a question?" I said."What do you have against me?"

' "Like I said on the beach, you're a newspaperman," he said.

' "So?"

' "You get in people's business when they don't want you to get in their business."

' "I look for news that people want to read."

' "And you think I'm news, don't you?"

' "Aren't you? You're from the West. You're good with a gun, or so I keep hearing. And now I find out you're not supposed to return to the West. Something about an agreement. Yes, it sounds like news."

' "No, Mr Stokesbury, it sounds like you trying to get in my business. If you come with us, just stay out of the way."

'Early the next morning the three of us left. Thus my sojourn on Jekyll Island was brief but memorable. In Savannah we stopped long enough for me to send a telegraph to Stanley Wilcox. I didn't wait for a reply. We headed north where we could board the Union Pacific. And so here we are. I'm still chasing after a mystery. From the mystery will come an article that, I hope, my editor will appreciate, an article that my readers will love. I feel I can almost grab hold of it, but it keeps eluding me. That's the way it is with some stories. You just have to keep chasing. You can't give up. Henry Grady once told me that. And when Henry Grady gave advice, you paid attention.'

CHAPTER 19

Eloise listened and then pulled pages of notes from her desk drawer. She handed them to Marcus. He was confused, but he began to read. Her scribbling was illegible.

'Eloise, forgive me, but your handwriting is atrocious.'

She took the pages and tossed them back into the drawer.

'I like a mystery too,' she said. 'I have contacts here in the West that you don't have. Some are in Missouri.'

'So you think you've learned something about Ezra,' Owen said.

He came out of the back room with two cups of coffee in one hand and one cup in the other. From the look of the scowl on his face, he was not pleased.

'I'm pretty sure I have,' she said. 'He used to ride with Jesse and Frank James. The story I've heard is that he was the fastest, deadliest gun in the gang. That helps to explain what he did during the train robbery. He himself had some experience with train robberies. But he decided to give it all up. He left the gang long before the Northfield robbery, which was a good thing. After Jesse was killed, Ezra disappeared. Nobody knew what happened to him. I telegraphed one man who replied that I was wrong. He said there was no way Ezra McPherson could be in Cheyenne. He said he was dead.

Maybe he is dead. Maybe he's just a ghost. Is he a ghost, Mr Chesterfield?'

Owen sipped the coffee.

'Damn, I make a good cup of coffee,' he said. 'No, Miss Endicott, he is not a ghost. I don't think a ghost could handle a Colt .45 the way he does.'

'The folks I know in Missouri couldn't tell me exactly what happened to Ezra. Somehow I think you know all about it. In fact, I think you were probably right in the middle of it.'

'There are things I cannot tell you.'

'So Ezra rode with the James gang,' Marcus said. 'And then after Jesse was killed, he disappeared, vanished – and later showed up on Jekyll Island. I'm beginning to understand. There was an agreement. Old man Tisdale said Ezra couldn't return to the West. That must have been part of the agreement. It must have been – if Ezra left Missouri for good, he could never return to the West. And who offered the agreement? Who offered Ezra shelter from the violence that plagued Missouri? It was you, Owen. After Jesse's murder, the railroads and the banks feared Ezra would ride again, would seek vengeance.'

'I'm not confirming anything you say,' Owen said. 'But I will tell you this – he is willing to put his life in danger to help Luke. He cares for that boy like a father cares for a son.'

'So Ezra is in danger,' Marcus said.

'The Swearingen foreman, Rayburn,' Eloise said. 'He's from Missouri.'

'Yes, ma'am, indeed he is.'

'I've been told he wanted to kill Ezra.'

'Ezra never turned his back to him,' Owen said.

'He even set a trap for him, on a lonely country road.'

'The men working for him weren't as good as Ezra,' Owen said.

'You think Rayburn will try again to kill him?' Marcus said.

'We need to get Ezra back on the Union Pacific heading East. The problem is he's got a soft spot in his heart for the homesteaders out here. He's willing to forsake safety, security. I'm afraid he's going to try to help them.'

'If he does, what will you do?' Eloise asked.

'I'll stand right there beside him, ma'am. I fought for the Union, and Ezra fought for the South. Some folks might think it strange that we're friends, but we are. He's an ornery cuss. But I know if I ever needed his help, I'd get it. If he's in the middle of a range war, then I'll be in the middle of it too. I want to ask a favour of both of you. You know a lot about Ezra McPherson. But don't print it. At least not now. Perhaps later, much later. You see, there are plenty of young men who would like to try to kill the fastest gun in the James gang.'

Marcus and Eloise did not answer, but Owen did not worry. He needed no answer. He looked at their faces and knew they would honour his request.

'There's more to this story,' Marcus said. 'I keep asking myself – why are you and Ezra such good friends? I think I've figured it out. It was probably the night before he left Missouri. Knowing Ezra the little I know him, I imagine he took a few days to decide if he wanted to accept your offer. As the days passed, people wondered when he was going to avenge Jesse's murder. I imagine Rayburn was afraid. But Ezra did nothing. He made up his mind and gave you his decision. He packed all the things he'd need, which wasn't much. He probably wanted to bid farewell to a neighbour, someone he'd always liked, someone he'd always depended on, someone who had hid him when the law was on his trail. Maybe he had some livestock he wanted his neighbour to look after. And perhaps Rayburn would know that Ezra wanted to say good-bye to a friend he'd never see again. By this time Rayburn had had enough time to assemble a group of men. And so he arranged for some of his men to lie in wait along that country road. Someone who knew of the ambush, one of Rayburn's associates, talked about it in a saloon. He talked about the last day Ezra would spend on this earth, and you happened to be in the saloon. You needed a drink, to settle your nerves, because what you were doing was risky. Getting Ezra out of Missouri might not be so easy. After all, Rayburn wanted him dead. He didn't want to spend the rest of his life looking over his shoulder, expecting to see Ezra taking dead aim. And so you heard the man talk, maybe even joke, about the ambush. I can see it now. You didn't even finish your drink. You hurried out of the saloon and headed for Ezra's place. He was already gone down that lonely country road. You chased after him. You caught up with him before the gunfire started, or maybe it had already started. You helped Ezra fight his way out of the ambush. You risked your life to save his.'

'Marcus, I am truly impressed,' Eloise said.

'Owen, am I correct? In the ambush that was supposed to kill him, Ezra was not alone, was he?'

Owen grinned and sipped the coffee and set the cup on the top of Eloise's desk.

'No, Stokesbury, he was not alone,' Owen said. 'He had a span of mules with him.'

Ezra saw them when they were still surrounded by the darkness. Riders – perhaps a half dozen. They slowed their horses, and Ezra pulled his pistol and held it next to the saddle horn. Even when the men drew near, he could not see their faces.

'You're out mighty late, mister,' one of the men said.

'So are you.'

'What's your business out here?'

'My business is none of yours, sonny.'

'It is if you're on Swearingen land, and you're on Swearingen land.'

'Well, you have my deepest apologies.'

'Just who the hell are you?'

'The name's McPherson.'

'He's the man who stopped the train robbery,' one of the others said.

'Yeah, let's just let him go.'

'Treutlin, it ain't worth a fight.'

The fellow named Treutlin apparently was the leader. If it came to a fight, Ezra figured he would take him down first.

'I hear you're awfully good with a gun.'

'Good enough, I reckon,' Ezra said. 'What have you boys been up to?'

'Calling on some of our neighbours. Just letting them know this is no place for them.'

'That was real hospitable of you. Have you boys ever been in a range war? It can get awfully nasty.'

'We can handle ourselves. Just how fast are you?'

Treutlin reached for his pistol but stopped. Ezra held his .45 on him.

'I don't want to kill you, sonny, but I will if I have to. You boys ride back to the rock you crawled out from under. And don't look back. If you do, you'll never do it again.'

They spurred their horses and rode past Ezra. Soon they returned to the darkness.

'I'm sure I'll meet up with that bunch again,' he said.

Slowly he rode across the prairie to Cheyenne. The few cottonwoods he passed swayed in the breeze, and the breeze brought the whispers of war, a voice he knew all too well. Once again he was a part of it. He could not escape it. War called from the hilltops and the valleys, from parched grasslands and clear rivers. He stopped. Before him, Cheyenne lay asleep in the early morning. The eastern sky already burned red. War beckoned. The eastbound Union Pacific would leave without him.